The Waikiki Hummer
A Waikiki Hummer Adventure – Book 1
Shannon Stiles

Table of Contents

The Waikiki Hummer (Waikiki Hummer Adventures, #1) 1
Foreword 3
Chapter 1..4
Chapter 2..8
Chapter 3..12
Chapter 4..17
Chapter 5..20
Chapter 6..25
Chapter 7..29
Chapter 8..32
Chapter 9..36
Chapter 10..40
Chapter 11..45
Chapter 12..49
Chapter 13..53
Chapter 14..58
Chapter 1..64
Chapter 2..70
Chapter 3..74
Chapter 4..77

Disclaimer

This book contains adult language and *very* explicit sexual content. It is not intended for nor suitable for anyone under the age of 18, nor for those who find this type of material offensive. If you fall into either of these two categories, please do NOT read this.

The Waikiki Hummer

Foreword

Terry Jean Rollins – TJ to her friends and The Waikiki Hummer to the rest of the world – is a cute, blonde, 23-year-old resident of Honolulu with only one ambition in life, to suck the cocks of as many shy, middle-aged, dorky male visitors to Waikiki as she can. She is a self-confessed dork lover who considers herself to be "maybe the best cocksucker in the entire world!" and dick-draining dorky tourists is her hobby. These are her stories, every one of them 110% true, according to her.

Chapter 1

He was sitting in the center section of the bus, alone, leaning against the window, looking sad and forlorn, wearing horned-rim glasses and a really dorky-looking crew cut. *And,* there was a wedding ring on his finger. Perfect. Just what I was looking for.

Probably on his way to Ala Moana Center, I judged as I walked down the aisle toward him. When I got there, I said, "Mind if I sit next to you?" and flashed my friendliest smile.

He scooted over to give me more room, probably thinking it was odd I chose to sit next to him, since the bus was practically empty. But he said, "Fine," and smiled back at me.

I slid in beside him. "Here on vacation?" I said.

"Business. You?"

"I live here," I said.

"Lucky you." The way he said it made it sound as though his visit to Honolulu had so far been less than pleasurable. Given the chance, I hoped to change all that for him.

"Where you from?"

"Colorado. Denver."

"It sounds like you're not enjoying yourself here in our beautiful city."

"It's all right."

"How about your wife?" I pointed at his wedding ring. "I'll bet she likes it."

"She's not here. It's just me. Here on business."

Excellent! "How long is it, anyway?" I said.

He gave me a funny look. "What?"

"How long? Your business trip?"

"Oh. Two weeks. One more to go." He repeated the look. I couldn't quite tell what it meant. Apprehension, perhaps? Or maybe lust. I am, after all, not *that* bad looking. I wouldn't describe myself as beautiful – cute would probably be a better description. I've heard guys call me that. "She's a really cute girl," they'd say. And I think I agree with them. I *am* cute. I've got perky tits and a shapely ass and a really *friendly*-looking smile.

"I'm TJ," I said, and offered my hand.

"George," he said, shaking it with a slightly-damp palm.

When he released my hand, I let it drop down and land on his left thigh, just a few inches from his lap. He flinched slightly but left it there. I gave his thigh a tiny, almost-imperceptible squeeze.

"What do you like to do for excitement. George? What turns you on?" I flashed him that friendly smile once again.

"I play chess."

Excitement? Chess? That wasn't the kind of answer I'd been expecting.

"And golf. I'm a really good golfer."

Ooh, more excitement. "Really?"

"Yup. I've even won a couple of tournaments."

"You don't say." I gave his thigh another squeeze – a little harder this time – and slid my hand a couple of inches closer to his crotch. He looked down at it but didn't complain.

"What about you, TJ?"

"Me?"

"Yeah. What do you do for excitement? What are your hobbies?"

This conversation wasn't heading in the direction I'd intended. My new friend, George, seemed to be a little slow on the uptake. I decided I needed to be more direct. "I only have one hobby," I told him.

"And? What is it?"

I turned and leaned closer to him and put my mouth up close to his ear. Then, in my best sexy-sounding voice, I whispered, "I like to suck cock." As I said it, I switched hands on his thigh and slid my left hand the rest of the way up his thigh, into his crotch, and grabbed his cock through his pants. Surprise, surprise – it was already rock-hard. Maybe George wasn't as slow as he seemed.

His eyebrows shot up about 14 inches. "What?" he said, turning to look at me.

"I like to pick up strange men – almost always tourists – and go to their hotel with them and then give them the best blowjob they've ever had in their entire life. It's my specialty. Blowjobs." I smiled and squeezed his cock several more times.

"How much?" George said.

"What?" I didn't understand the question.

"How much do you charge?"

I pulled my head back and gave him my best *disappointed* look. "Really, George? You think I'm a hooker? Look at me. Look at how I'm dressed." My outfit of the day consisted of white shorts, a baby-blue T-shirt and rubber *zoris* instead of shoes.

"Have you seen the hookers in this town, George? They're cruising Waikiki every night, strolling up and down Kalakaua, asking tourists if they'd like a *date*. Their skirts are four inches long and the heels of their shoes are twice that."

"I've seen 'em." he said.

I squeezed his cock again – hard, this time – and didn't release it for several seconds. "It's a hobby with me, George. I just like sucking dick. It makes me feel ... oh, I don't know. Powerful, I guess." *Yeah. Taking that stiff dick and turning it into a soft little lump of flesh with the consistency of a limp dishcloth, it makes me feel powerful.*

"I see."

"And I especially like strange men."

"Strange? You think I'm strange?"

"Not strange weird. Strange like we don't know each other."

"Oh."

"So, ...?"

"No charge?"

"Nope."

"All right. I'm up for it," he said.

"Obviously," I said, pointing at his pants, which now featured a tent where the fly was. "You'd better carry something in front of that when we get off the bus."

"I'll do that." He smiled, picked his briefcase up off the floor and held it up for me to see.

"Perfect," I told him.

Chapter 2

The hotel where George was staying was not one of the fancy, beachfront, super-expensive tourist traps fronting Kalakaua Avenue with back doors that open up right onto the beach. I guess I should have expected that, since George had said he was here on business, not as a tourist. Anyway, it was on a side street, almost three blocks up from the beach, near Ala Wai Boulevard and the canal.

We had to hail a cab after we got off the bus. George's hotel was back down at the other end of Waikiki, the Diamond Head end. The driver who stopped to pick us up wasn't too happy about the fact we were only going a few blocks but George promised him a big tip and when we got there, he gave him a twenty and told him to keep the change. The cabbie thanked us and drove off with an extra-large smile on his face.

George's room was on the ninth floor, with a view of Ala Wai Boulevard, Ala Wai Canal, and the Ala Wai Golf Course on the other side of the canal. With the exception of the lanai – which I doubted got much use because of the constant winds swirling around this area – it was just a standard hotel room like you might find in any business hotel in any large city. There was a double bed, a desk and chair, a dresser, an armchair, a medium-size flat-screen TV and, of course, a bathroom and a place to hang clothes. Nothing fancy, but then, we weren't here for the décor, anyway.

"What now?" George said, turning to face me.

"Why don't you take off some of those clothes? Honolulu's too hot to be wearing a suit."

"Yeah, you're right. It *is* hot." He started removing his clothes, tossing them onto the armchair while at the same time casting nervous glances in my direction.

"Relax, George," I told him, adding a slight chuckle. "I'm not going to hurt you. I'm not going to rob you or yell rape or anything like that. I just want to suck your cock. It's my hobby, it's what I do for fun."

"Strange hobby," he said.

He had stripped down to just his boxer shorts and socks by this time and was trying to remove his socks by hopping on one foot while he pulled a sock off the other foot. It wasn't going that well – he was hopping all over the room, trying to maintain his balance. When he hopped by me, I reached out and pushed him over backwards, onto the bed, and pulled off both socks for him.

"Thanks," he said, looking up at me from his recumbent position.

"Wouldn't want you to hurt yourself before we get to the fun part." I hopped up on the bed and slid up close to him, with my head on his right shoulder and my right arm draped over his chest. "Comfy?" I said.

"Uh-huh."

"Good." I stretched my head up and began to nibble on his right ear. At the same time my right hand slithered down his body until it landed on top of his once-again-rock-hard cock, but outside his boxer shorts. I let it rest there, separated from his dick by just a thin layer of cotton, without doing anything – no squeezing, no stroking, nothing – while I continued to chew on his ear.

He shivered.

"Relax, George. You're gonna like this. I promise."

"I think I already like it."

"It gets better," I said. I slipped my hand under the waistband of his shorts and wrapped my fingers around his dick, giving it a couple of light squeezes – what I like to think of as *introductory* squeezes or *How do you do?* squeezes.

George moaned and said, "Fuck, that feels good!"

"Take off your shorts," I told him.

He reached down and, with just a little help from me, slipped his boxers down over his hips and onto his legs, from where he kicked them off. His cock – six inches of thick, beautiful man-meat – stared up at me, wavering up and down, practically wearing a *Please hurry up and do me* sign. I smiled, thinking *that's what I'm here for,* leaned down and sucked that beautiful purple-headed shaft into my mouth.

George seemed to like that. I swirled my tongue slowly around the head of his dick, occasionally licking upward on the bottom of the shaft, only to concentrate again on the head. Any girl who's sucked a few cocks will tell you that's where the action is – the dickhead. The shaft is really only there so you'll have something to hang onto while you're working on the head.

Apparently, though, it had been a long while since George had been laid or gotten his dick gobbled, because I was just getting started, just warming up, when I felt his cock go super-hard and begin to spasm. I put my tongue on the bottom of his dickhead, wiggled it back and forth slowly, and began to gently suck.

A warm stream of cum – my tasty reward, as I usually liked to think of it – spurted out onto my tongue, followed by a slight pause and then two more spasmodic ejections. I sucked it all up and swallowed, never letting go of his dick. But it wasn't just George's dick doing the spasm thing. His whole body shook and he arched his back each time he pumped a load into my mouth. He commented out loud on it, too. He went, "Oh! Oh! Oh!' and "Oh!"

I spit his dick out into my hand and hung onto it, massaging it gently as I watched him gasping for air, trying to catch his breath. He really wasn't in the best of shape for a guy – what, forty or fifty years old? The thought crossed my mind I might have some explaining to do if old George had a heart attack and croaked on me.

"Shit! I'm so sorry," he said when he was able to breathe normally again.

"Don't worry about it," I said, laughing. "We're not finished yet."

"No?"

"No." Actually, this – getting a load of warm jizz shot into my mouth 30 seconds or so after I start sucking a strange guy's cock – happened to me a lot. But I was never disappointed. I liked to think it was because I was such a skillful cocksucker I could get any guy to cum in record time. And also, I knew we were just getting started. If George thought that shooting one little load of cum down my throat was the end of this adventure, he was in for a big, big surprise.

I've always thought of cocksucking as an art form, something to be done slowly and gracefully, leisurely, sensually stroking and licking your way toward a tasty treat until a stream of warm, delicious cum – the reward – fills your mouth and rolls down your throat. When done right, it can take hours, with the reward being repeated two and sometimes three times, until that poor, pitiful penis is completely wasted, of no good to any woman for several days. And that's what I intended to do to George – suck his cock so dry it would be useless for the next week or so!

Chapter 3

I let George rest while I entertained myself playing with his dick and giving it an occasional wet, slurpy lick, just to keep him interested. When I was younger, I used to wish I was a boy so I'd have a dick to play with whenever I wanted, but as I got older I realized that wasn't necessary. Any reasonably decent-looking girl could pretty much find a cock to play with any time she wanted. Usually, all you had to do was ask.

After 15 or 20 minutes of me diddling with it, George's dick had re-inflated to a sort of floppy, spongy fullness – not really hard but on its way. During the entire time, he only said two things to me, "I like that," and "Are you for sale? I want to buy you and take you home with me." The rest of the time he just moaned.

I thought I knew a way to speed things up. I used my hand to milk his cock for a minute or two, then leaned over, put it in my mouth and began massaging the tip – just the top part of his dickhead – with my tongue. At the same time I began to hum.

"What the hell?" George propped himself up on both elbows and gazed at me, looking slightly alarmed. "What are you doing?"

I pulled his cock out of my mouth, making an exaggerated smacking sound as I did so. "Round two," I told him.

"No, I mean that noise. That buzzing sound. What was that?"

Keeping George's cock in my hand, I sat back on my haunches. "I was humming."

A puzzled look slid across his face, replacing the alarm. "Why?"

I shrugged. "I like it. It's my thing. I like to hum while I suck cock."

"You're kidding!"

"Nope." To prove it to him, I leaned forward, popped his dick back into my mouth, and hit him with about 20 seconds of the Australian folk song, *Waltzing Matilda*. When I spit his dick back out into my hand, it was quite a bit firmer than when it had gone in. Also larger. "See? Guys like it, too," I said.

"Is it always that song?" he asked me.

"Nope. I mix 'em up. Why? You got a favorite song you want me to hum for you?"

"Yeah. *In the Still of the Night.*"

"Shit, how old *are* you, anyway? Damn, George, that song's like a hundred years old."

"I know, but I can't help it. I like fifties music. And that's one of my favorites. Do you know it?"

"The Five Satins, right?"

"Yeah."

"I think I do." I leaned back down and slurped his dick – still only at about half-mast but trying hard to make it up to the crow's nest – into my mouth, lightly sucking and tonguing the tip as I began to hum *In the Still of the Night.*

And then a funny thing happened. As I was working my tongue in a circular motion around the head of George's cock, humming his favorite song and forcing that cock into a more-rigid state, he began to sing along with me. Pretty loudly, in fact.

Trouble was, George wasn't much of a singer. In fact, he was fucking terrible! But I knew just the cure for that. I rolled over to one side and removed my shorts and panties, then climbed back on top of him. Temporarily abandoning his almost totally firmed-up dick for the moment, I crawled up his body until my crotch was about an inch from his face.

"You like pussy, George?" I asked him.

"I do."

"Take a good look, then. Freshly washed, carefully shaved, just a nice, clean, smooth, moist pussy, with no hair to get in your mouth and spoil that creamy goodness." I moved a little forward, grabbed him by the ears and gently pulled his head upward. Just a bit. Then I lowered my cunt – now juicy with anticipation – onto his waiting mouth, grinding it against his lips before releasing his ears and spreading open my pussy with my fingers to make sure his tongue would have easy access to my clit.

It was pretty obvious George had experience with this particular pastime – he knew exactly what to do. He grabbed me by the ass with both hands, pulling me down more tightly against him, then thrust his tongue into my slit, licking it with long, slow strokes up and down, always stopping at the top to swirl my clit with the tip of his tongue. It felt wonderful. I let him have five or six good licks and then I pulled back, sat up and smiled down at him.

"What's wrong?" he said.

"Nothing." I climbed off him and reversed my position, so that I was now facing away from him, and wiggled my cunt back into position onto his mouth. His dick was nice and stiff now and it bobbed up and down in front of me, inviting me to gobble it up. Or down. Or both. So I did.

It took longer this time. Of course, I anticipated that – I've done this before. You can't expect a guy who's just gifted you with a nice, creamy load to give you another present only a minute or two later. It takes a while. You have to work at it a little bit the second time. And the third. And the fourth, if you get that far, which doesn't happen very often.

So I worked at it. And while I licked and lapped and sucked my way around George's dick, he worked at keeping my pussy happy by doing the same – licking and lapping and sucking. He was good at it, too. Excellent, in fact.

Blowing a guy doesn't usually give me an orgasm. Neither does having my pussy tongue-fucked. At least, not one of those big, earth-shattering, body-shaking climaxes that many women seem to experience. Or like George's spasmodic spurting episode, earlier.

What happens to me is different – I get mini-orgasms, as I like to think of them. Over and over, lots of them. Sometimes, in the course of one of these 'sessions,' I'm rewarded with dozens of deliciously tingling mini-climaxes. While these are my favorites, I occasionally like a *big-time* orgasm, too. And the only way I ever get one of those is to slip a dick into my pussy and let it fuck me silly.

So, while George was doing an excellent job down there, grinding away on my pussy, I began to entertain the idea of fucking him. Although slurping dicks is kinda my specialty, a girl needs a good fuck occasionally, I told myself. And I was pretty sure old George could give me one.

Of course, that was against my self-imposed rule #1 – *Oral sex only. Never fuck any of the guys you pick up.* And I never did. Okay, make that *seldom.* I *seldom* fucked any of the guys I picked up. There are always exceptions. You know what they say – rules are made to be broken.

However, before I could make an exception for George, his cock started bucking and bouncing and dancing around in my mouth and I knew he was getting ready to cum. I'd spent too long thinking about fucking him and now it was too late. I released his cock from my mouth and, continuing to stroke it with my hand, turned my head back toward him and said, "How we doin' back there, Georgie boy?"

George's muffled voice answered back, "Oh! Oh! Oh!"

My feelings, exactly, George. I stuck his dick back into my mouth and resumed sucking on the head – just in time, too. It took only a couple of quick licks until I got my second reward, thinner and not as rich and creamy as the first time, but I swallowed it with just as much satisfaction. Maybe even more so, since the second load is almost always the last time it shoots out of a really firm dick. Any future rewards I might get would come from a spongy, semi-erect, possibly even *reluctant* cock. While that's okay, I guess, I really prefer to suck cum out of a stiffy.

I could hear George mumbling something into my pussy. I'd been grinding away, thinking only about how good it felt and not that I might be suffocating him back there behind me. It wouldn't be good form to leave a dead man behind, I decided, so I raised myself up onto my knees, leaned back and said, "What?"

He gulped fresh air for a few seconds, then raised his head and said, "Can you teach my wife to do that?"

"Probably not," I said, and lowered my pussy back onto his mouth. *And probably not really one of your better ideas, Georgie boy.*

Two hours later, George's dick was dead. I'd murdered it. It had been a really nice, friendly dick while it was still alive, but now it just lay there, all limp and sticky and gooey. Like all dead things, it was unable to move. And that meant our little adventure was over – it was time for me to split. I got up.

"Leaving?" George said, without looking up.

"Yup. Thanks for everything."

"Will I see you again?"

"Nope."

"Too bad," he said.

Yeah. Too bad, I silently agreed. In the history of my adventures as the legendary 'Waikiki Hummer,' this had been one of the better episodes. Old George had really come through. I gave him an A+ in pussy licking and stamina, and a strong A in everything else. Plus, he had a Goldilocks dick – not too big, not too small, just right.

I washed up and got dressed. George had already fallen asleep and I didn't want to wake him, so I whispered, "Bye, George," and let myself out, closing the door quietly behind me.

Chapter 4

According to social media, which, as everyone knows, is the most reliable source of news and information *anywhere*, I am either an urban myth or an urban legend, or perhaps even a secret advertising plot by the state of Hawaii, designed to lure men into visiting Waikiki. That last one always makes me smile, just thinking that little old me – the girl known all over the web as the Waikiki Hummer – could be responsible for bringing more male visitors to Hawaii.

Of course, there's also a faction that insists I do not exist and never have existed, that I'm just a fantasy some guy posted in a chat room one day and it got picked up and went viral. I know that's not true so I ignore those shitheads and concentrate on the positive – passing out blowjobs to random visitors and helping the tourism industry. Plus, it's a really enjoyable hobby – I *love* to suck cock!

I've been doing this – picking up guys and treating them to the best oral sex of their lives, if you believe the social media reviews – for a few years now. I'm 23 and I've been known as the Waikiki Hummer for almost three years, after voters at a well-known porn site voted me that name over the other choice, the Waikiki Gobbler. I was actually pretty happy about that. Hummer is a way better name than Gobbler. That sounds like a turkey. Besides, Hummer fits me better – I'm the girl who likes to hum.

I understand that same porn site is now offering a reward for pictures and/or video of me and any of my "legendary" performances. Hah! Good luck with that. I *never* let guys take pictures!

Anyway, after a somewhat awkward introduction to the world of blowjobs, I discovered that I loved the sensation of having of having a cock explode – not literally, of course – inside my mouth, then gradually shrink into a smaller, softer version of itself as I continued to suck on it. I also learned to be gentle as I sucked, because I found out recently-exploded dicks are sensitive. *Extremely* sensitive.

I was a late bloomer, I guess. The first time I ever had a cock in my mouth was the evening after my 19th birthday party. That cock was attached to a guy I'd known most of my life – Fred. As I look back at it now, I realize he basically mouth-raped me. One minute we were making out on my parents' lanai and he was fingering my pussy. I had my hand in his pants, rhythmically squeezing his cock on the way to one of my favorite sexual activities back then, giving hand jobs to my 'special' male friends. And the next thing I knew he'd grabbed me by the head, stuffed his cock in my mouth, and was unloading what appeared to be years of teenage horniness down my throat.

My reaction at the time was different than the way I feel now. I was pissed. I spit the cum I hadn't swallowed out onto the lanai and said, "What the fuck was that?"

Fred looked embarrassed and said something lame, like, "Sorry. I couldn't help myself." Then he buttoned up his jeans and went back into the house, leaving me alone on the chaise lounge.

It wasn't until later that night, as I was getting ready for bed, that I realized I'd actually kinda *enjoyed* what Fred had done to me. Maybe not so much the fact that he'd run off just when it seemed things were getting interesting, but the experience, itself – the feeling of power that came with that stiff cock starting to wilt in my mouth. *I did that,* I told my reflection in the bathroom mirror. And my reflection responded, *Yeah. But just think how much better it would be with us in control.*

So that's pretty much how it all began. I was talked into it by my evil mirror-image. I'm pretty sure a sweet, innocent girl like myself wouldn't be doing any of this stuff right now if it hadn't been for my reflection, that girl in the mirror, explaining to me how much fun we could have with dicks if *we* were the ones in charge, not the guy, and convincing me the easy way to accomplish that was to pick up male tourists. Which is what I did, almost exclusively, for the first couple of years. I'd pick up a guy in Waikiki – usually on the bus – take him somewhere and suck his dick until he cried uncle, then split, never to see him again. Anonymous sex, they call it, and I loved it!

That is and has been my preference – picking up male tourists in Waikiki. But once in a while I get a taste for something local, and when I do, I take a bus ride out into the boonies, to places where tourists don't go. I've found there are friendly dicks out there in the boonies, too.

Weren't you scared? I hear people asking. Oh, sure. It was scary the first time. Actually, it's scary *every* time, going up to a strange guy and trying to convince him to let you suck his cock, just for fun. There's always the chance he's going to turn you down, or call a cop, or maybe even start screaming for help. But that's part of the fun, the thrill of it, the danger. Who knows what might happen?

Anyway, in almost four years of doing this, I've only been turned down once, and he was nice about it. And there was a really good reason he turned me down, too. *Really* good. The guy was a Catholic priest dressed in civilian clothes.

I guess that's all you really need to know about me. I'm 23 years old, blonde hair, cute face, reasonable figure, and I like to think of myself as the best cocksucker in the whole fucking world!

That pretty much sums me up, except for one thing I neglected to mention and probably should have. I live with my boyfriend, Julien. He's from France and he has a really big nose. *Really* big. And he can use that nose to do wonderful ... well, I'll tell you about Julien some other time, 'cause he's not part of this story. All you need to know for now is that I'm not cheating on him. He approves of my hobby.

Chapter 5

A week or so after my latest tryst, I was horny and back on the prowl again, riding buses through Waikiki, looking for just the right type of guy. My choice was almost always a guy who resembled my last conquest. George had been near-perfect, what with those horned-rim glasses and that dorky 1950s style haircut.

Dorky. That's what I was searching for. That's my type – dorky, middle-age guys who have a certain look about them. The *look* is a little hard to describe but, basically, it's a cross between one of confusion – as if they were time-travelers who'd just arrived from some long-ago previous century and were totally fucking bewildered by what they now were experiencing – and resignation – *Oh, well, I'm here now and I might as well make the best of it and see what's going on.*

See? Hard to describe. But I recognize it when I see it. And there's actually more to it. The perfect dorky-looking guy also has a look of innocence about him, as if he could even be a 40-year-old virgin. And he certainly has never had a reasonably-hot girl he didn't know put his cock in her mouth and suck on it.

But then I saw these two guys sitting together. These guys were definitely *not* my type – they were young, muscular, and good-looking, both wearing tank tops and bathing suits, obviously together and just as obviously on their way to or from the beach. Neither of them even came close to qualifying for the *dorky* label. They were laughing and talking to one another and they both seemed happy, carefree, and confident.

I began thinking about a threesome. I'd never done a threesome before. Well, not with two guys, anyway. I'd done the other kind – one guy and two girls, and even once with three girls. Those were fun but, for my taste, there was too much pussy and not enough dick.

Two cocks in my mouth would be a dream come true. Not really, of course. I'd never thought that much about it and I didn't even know if I could fit two cocks into my mouth at the same time. But I'd certainly be willing to give it a try. My pussy started to dance and get moist as I thought about it.

I considered the logistics of that – what position I'd have to be in to do it, for example – and the more I thought about it, two dicks at once didn't seem that practical. I'd probably have to alternate between them, I decided, first slurping one delicious cock and then the other, back and forth, back and forth. And to make this vision of yummy goodness come true, all I had to do was figure out how to approach those guys and talk them into an afternoon of fun and games. With one guy, that usually wasn't too difficult. It would probably work with two, as well, was my guess.

I was just getting up my nerve to go talk to them when one of them reached up and pulled the stop cord, signaling they intended to get off at the next stop. If I was going to do anything about the fantasy building in my head, the time had come to make my move. I took a deep breath and edged over closer to the aisle, preparing to get up, but before I could, both guys slid out of their seats and stood up.

As soon as I saw them, standing there in the aisle, I realized my fantasy was extremely unlikely to work out the way I'd intended. How did I come to that conclusion? They were holding hands as they started down the aisle toward the front door. I stared longingly after them as they got off the bus – two lovers on their way to the beach. I wondered if I could convince them to – oh, too late. The bus was moving again.

Shit! That was disappointing. All juiced up and no one to play with. I suppose that's how I ended up here in this hotel room with Tony, a guy who didn't even come close to my ideal *type*.

Tony was on that bus, too. And when the two guys left – greatly disappointing me, I might add – I looked around and saw him, sitting alone about five rows behind me. A long way from perfect, I told myself, glancing back at him, but certainly better than nothing. He caught me checking him out and smiled back at me.

That smile immediately removed him from the category known in my head as *shy, dorky guys who look like they've never been laid.* Tony wasn't anything like the guys I consider my ideal type. He was big and muscular, wearing a tight black T-shirt so you'd notice those muscles, and he had black, slicked-back hair. He looked Italian. Or maybe Greek. You know what I mean – just a little toward the *dark* side of the Caucasian spectrum. If you'd asked me to speculate on his occupation, I probably would have guessed he was an East Coast gangster.

Still, like I said, something is better than nothing, so now here I was, naked on a bed in a hotel room with Tony's cock in my mouth, humming Billy Joel's *New York State of Mind* at Tony's request. At least, as much of it as I knew.

"That's it, baby. Suck. And hum. Suck and hum." And then he went, "Ooh, ... ooh, ... ooh."

I thought he was getting ready to cum, so I did as he asked. I sucked and I hummed and I twirled my tongue around the head of his dick and I pumped my hand up and down his shaft like he was a cow and I was milking him. His dick started dancing around in my mouth and I thought, *This is it. He's going to cum.*

But he didn't. Instead, he pulled his cock out of my mouth, flipped me over onto my stomach, and pulled my legs apart.

Ooh, doggy style, I remember thinking. Not my favorite, but I supposed we could always proceed to something that was more clitoris-friendly.

However, doggy style was not what Tony had in mind. He pulled me up to my knees, spread my butt cheeks apart, pushed my face and upper body down onto the mattress and stuck his cock, all wet and juicy from being in my mouth, in my ass. Just like that – no warning, no *How do you do, ma'am? I'll just be inspecting your backdoor plumbing today, if you don't mind,* no nothing. Just jammed it in there without an invitation.

"Owwwww," I said.

"Relax, sweetheart. You're gonna like this."

That was doubtful. I've had a cock up my ass before – twice, in fact – and I didn't like it either time. It hurt. And I didn't even agree to let this guy fuck my pussy, much less my ass. This was supposed to be about a blowjob.

He was pumping away, just like my asshole was a cunt instead of the delicate flower it actually is, but before I could protest or struggle to free myself, Tony went into his *ooh, ... ooh, ... ooh, I'm gonna cum* routine again. That was quick – buttfucking was obviously his thing. I was sure he was going to cum this time and I was right. He did, but not in my ass. At the last second, he pulled his dick out and shot a humongous load onto my back, covering it in warm cum that leaked down my sides and tickled my ribs. Like I said, a *humongous* load. I felt like I'd just starred in a porn video.

"That was great, babe," he said, shaking his dick, then climbing off me and slapping me on the ass. "I'm gonna take a shower. You're welcome to join me. You can show me that humming trick again."

"Yeah, okay. I'll be there in a little bit," I said, without looking at him. "After I catch my breath."

"Suit yourself." He went into the bathroom and closed the door.

Obviously I had made a bad decision this time, deviating from my preferred type to pick up a fuckhead like Tony. But I'd learned a valuable lesson – straying from type was dangerous. In the future, I'd be sure to limit my adventures to those dorky types I liked so well. And as for Tony, well, he deserved to learn a lesson, too.

I turned my head and stared at the bathroom door. "You're gonna be sorry you did that, you fucking bastard!" I said quietly. "Nobody fucks Terry Jean Rollins in the ass without an invitation and gets away with it!"

Chapter 6

When I heard the shower door close and the water start, I climbed off the bed and went looking for something with which to wipe myself off. I found just what I was looking for hanging from a hanger in an alcove near the front door – a new, never-worn, dressy aloha shirt, the fancy kind businessmen here wear to their offices on Aloha Fridays. It still had the price tag attached to it, showing the pre-tax price of $129.95. Nice, but Waikiki-priced. You can get the identical item downtown for about 75 bucks. I pulled it off the hanger and used it to clean Tony's cum off my back.

On the floor beneath the hanging clothes I found another useful-looking item, a twelve-inch-high statuette of a naked Hawaiian girl standing on a large rock, her hands spiraling above her head, making it look as if she was dancing. They sell these things in little stores all up and down Waikiki, sometimes labeling them as *genuine hand-carved lava-rock statues*. Actually, they're made out of some black synthetic liquid that they just pour into molds.

I picked it up. It was fairly heavy for such a small item, maybe three or four pounds, and hard as a rock, which, of course, it was supposed to be. I took it with me when I went back into the room, collected my clothes, and got dressed. Then I sat on the edge of the bed and waited for Tony to finish his shower.

The water stopped and the shower door opened and closed, followed by the sound of whistling as he dried himself off. *New York State of Mind*, of course. I went over and stood by the door, taking the statuette with me.

A couple of minutes went by and then Tony emerged from the bathroom in a cloud of steam, naked and drying his hair with a towel. I leaned back against the wall and watched as he dropped the towel around his shoulders, squinted at the bed through the steam, and said, "Hey, babe. Where are you? You didn't leave, did you?"

That's when I hit him. I grabbed that little Hawaiian dancing girl statue by her spiraling arms, held it like a baseball bat, and swung the base into the side of Tony's head as hard as I could. As I did, I imagined I was a major league player, trying to hit a home run. You have to swing hard if you want to hit a home run!

Evidently, Tony's head was nearly as hard as my dancing girl weapon. His hand shot up to his ear, which was gushing blood, and he turned to look at me. "What the fuck?!!!" he said.

I took a step forward and hit him again, this time flush in the middle of his forehead. He didn't have much to say this time. His right hand instinctively reached out to grab me, but as it did, I stepped to the side and he kept right on going, collapsing face-first onto the floor, down for the count, as they say in boxing.

"How's that feel, Tony?" I said to the unconscious figure on the floor in front of me. "You're lucky I don't stick this fucking statue up *your* ass!" I eyed the statuette, still in my hand, and Tony's ass, peering up at me from the floor, while I considered whether or not that was possible.

In the end, I decided it would be too difficult. Anyway, I'd already come up with a better plan, a way of making Tony pay for his crime that sounded like a lot more fun than sticking something up his butt. I set about putting my plan into action.

The first step was finding Tony's suitcase. That was easy because it was right there in the room, over by the dresser. A nice, expensive-looking one, too. I put it on the bed and opened it. It was empty.

Not for long, I thought. I went around the room and collected every possession of Tony's I could find. His underwear and socks from the dresser, the shirts and pants hanging in the alcove, his watch and wallet and keys and phone and key card to the room – I grabbed them all and stuffed them into the suitcase, with the exception of the wallet, phone, and the key card. I stuck those in my pocket.

Tony continued to snooze on the floor. It was when I was getting his shoes from under the bed that I discovered the paper. Two reams of it, inside a small, canvas tote bag, wrapped in light blue paper with no identifying markings on the outside. That was a little odd. I didn't know why he needed two reams of paper, but it didn't really matter. If it was his, it was going into the suitcase, along with the shoes. I put the tote bag on the bed.

The suitcase was already pretty full by this time but I managed to jam the shoes into it. There was no room for the two reams of paper, though, so I left them on the bed while I forced the case closed. Then, after checking to make sure I had the key card in my pocket and that Tony was still breathing – he was – I dragged the suitcase down to the end of the hall, next to the elevators, where there was a rubbish chute.

That's what all this stuff of yours is now, Tony, I thought. *Just rubbish.* I opened the suitcase and proceeded to dump each item in it down the chute – clothes, watch, keys, just about everything Tony had except for his phone, wallet, and key card, which were in my pocket, and the statue and the two reams of paper, neither of which would fit into the suitcase and were still in the room.

I took out the wallet, opened it and looked inside. It was thick with twenty-dollar bills, which I decided would be a terrible waste to just throw away, so I pulled them out and stuffed them into my pocket. The wallet and the rest of its contents – license, credit cards, a photo of a naked, redheaded girl showing me her snatch, all of it – went down the chute.

The suitcase was too big to fit into the chute so I left it there, knowing someone would find it and give it a good home, and went back to the room. Tony was still asleep. It was easy to understand why – he'd had a rough day.

A final sweep of the room revealed I had left no incriminating evidence behind. In fact, I hadn't left much of anything behind – nothing of mine and nothing of Tony's. Basically, the only things left in the room were Tony's naked, unconscious body, the naked Hawaiian girl statue, and the tote bag with the two reams of paper, resting on the bed. I decided to take the statue and the paper, too. Leaving them behind would have made my revenge seem, well, ... incomplete.

Only one step remained in my plan – my *diabolical* plan, as I liked to think of it. I used the room phone to call the front desk and when the desk clerk answered, I put my hand over my mouth, deepened my voice and said, "Help! Help me!" Then I put the phone down without hanging it up and left, leaving the door slightly ajar.

As I stood at the end of the hall, waiting for an elevator, I decided that carrying the key card to Tony's room around with me probably wasn't that great of an idea, so I dumped that down the rubbish chute, as well. The elevator announced its arrival with a loud *ding*. The doors opened and two security guards rushed out, one saying to the other, "Which way? Which way?" I wanted to point down the hall, and then stick around to see what would happen when the guards found Tony, naked and unconscious from a head wound, but I couldn't, of course. So I got on the elevator and pushed the button that said *Lobby*.

Two minutes later I was strolling down sunny Kalakaua Avenue, feeling pretty good, carrying the tote bag with the paper and statuette in it and humming *New York State of Mind* softly to myself. Damn! That fucking song was stuck in my head and I knew every time I heard it, for the rest of my life, I'd be reminded of that scumbag, Tony, and what he did to me. Of course, I'd also be reminded of what I did to him, and that brought a smile to my face.

Chapter 7

When I got home, I put the two reams of paper in the bedroom, next to my printer, then washed the blood – Tony's blood, now dry – off the naked dancing girl statuette. After trying several locations, I finally settled on a shelf by the TV for the statue. Julien was gonna like that when he sees it – he likes anything having to do with naked women. I'll probably tell him I saw it and bought it for him. I'm sure he'd prefer hearing that rather than how I really got it.

My back felt a little sticky so I went in and took a long, hot shower – so long, in fact, that the water started getting cold. Normally, that would really piss off Julien, coming home to find no hot water for a shower, but he and some tourist babe he met were off fucking up a storm on Maui, or the Big Island, or one of the neighbor islands. He told me where they were going but I don't remember. It's not a big thing – he fucks who he wants and I fuck who I want. Or, more likely, I suck them off. That's our arrangement.

After heating up some leftovers for dinner, I turned on the evening news, wondering if they might have a story about a naked guy beaten unconscious in a Waikiki hotel room. They didn't. Not too surprising, really – stories that could scare away tourists seldom make the local news.

I watched TV for a while, then went to bed early. It had been a tough day in some ways. Tony had tricked me out of getting my reward – him pumping a load of warm, delicious cum into my mouth – and I was left feeling horny and frustrated. I'd wanted to feel that cock going limp in my mouth and know that it was me who'd temporarily hung an *Out of Order* sign on it, and now all that was left to me was masturbation. Trouble is, while I'm pretty good at jerking off a guy, I'm not that good at getting myself off. I really only like to rub my pussy when I have a dick in my mouth.

It didn't matter. I fell asleep before anything more than a fantasy could happen, and slipped into a sexy dream where I was *entertaining* a couple of distinguished-looking, middle-aged, bespectacled and extremely dorky medical researchers. The next thing I knew the sun was shining in my eyes, waking me. I lay there for a while, thinking about those researchers and trying to get myself back into a sexy mood. It didn't work, though, so I got up and got dressed and took a walk.

Julien and I live in a one-bedroom apartment down at the Diamond Head end of Waikiki. It isn't much, but it's what we can afford – living in Honolulu is super-expensive. It's also convenient to Kapahulu Avenue, a more-or-less main drag leading from Waikiki up toward Kaimuki, a Honolulu neighborhood some three miles away.

Afraid I might bump into Tony if I went into the heart of Waikiki, I headed up Kapahulu in the opposite direction, toward Kaimuki. I was looking for one of those little side-street stores where I could buy some food – there wasn't much to eat back at the apartment. There never was. Both Julien and I hate grocery shopping.

I found what I was looking for a short block or so past the Ala Wai Golf Course – a small shop not much bigger than the living room in my apartment, full of healthy goodies. I scooped up cups of instant ramen, a frozen pizza, a dozen chocolate cupcakes, two large bottles of Coke and a package of Tums, dumping them on the counter in front of an elderly clerk who eyed me with a mixture of amusement and suspicion.

"You eat good," she told me as she rang up the items on a cash register that looked to be at least 50 years old.

She was Korean. I could tell by her accent. There are lots of Korean people in Honolulu these days, many of them, it seems, running small stores like this one. They're the most recent major ethnic group to emigrate to Hawaii.

I grinned at her. "I can't cook," I confessed.

She smiled back. "Me, too," she said.

We stood there, smiling at each other, as she loaded my purchases into the tote bag – Tony's tote bag – that I'd brought with me. The total came to $22.78.

There had been $240 in nice, crisp, fresh-from-the-bank twenties in Tony's wallet yesterday and, as I said then, there was no good reason to let that cash go to waste when I threw the wallet away. Which is why $100 of it was now in my pocket, ready to pay for the items I'd just purchased. I reached into my pocket, pulled out two twenties and handed them to the still-smiling woman across the counter from me.

And that's when the trouble began. My new Korean friend looked at the two bills, then at me, then back at the twenties again. She held one of them up to a light above her counter, carefully studying it before turning it over and doing the same to the other side. She then put the first bill down and repeated the procedure with the second one I'd given her. Finally, she looked at me and said, "This no good."

"What?" I said, thinking I'd misunderstood her. She did have a heavy accent.

"Fake. This money no good."

"What!!"

"You stay," she said. "I tell Min Sung." She grabbed the two bills and hurried toward the back of the store, where she disappeared through a curtained doorway.

Fake? Tony's money was fake? Shit! Despite the clerk ordering me to stay, I decided not to stick around and see what Min Sung thought about all this. I snatched my tote bag off the counter and ran out the door, running as fast as I could back down Kapahulu toward Waikiki. Being arrested as a counterfeiter was not on my *to do* list for the day.

Chapter 8

Nobody chased me as I hurried down Kapahulu, back toward the safety of my apartment, but I still ran most of the way. The tote bag was a problem. It was too heavy and no matter which hand I held it in, it kept slamming against the side of my leg and made running difficult. I solved that minor complication as I ran by the golf course.

A couple of young guys were standing there, leaning against the chain-link fence and watching the golfers while they enjoyed an early-morning toke or two of marijuana. I stopped, took the two bottles of coke out of the tote bag and placed them on the ground by the fence. "Here. Have a drink on me, guys," I said as I ran off.

"Hey! Where ya going?" one of the guys called after me. "Have a smoke."

Under other circumstances, I might have taken him up on that offer – I really like weed. But right now I was in a hurry to get off the street. For all I knew, cops could be cruising up and down Kapahulu right now, in search of that dangerous counterfeiter known as … *me!* So I kept running.

By the time I got home, I was exhausted. I put the pizza in the freezer and flopped onto the living room couch, just lying there in a semi-reclining position, sucking in delicious oxygen until I could breathe normally again. When I'd regained my strength, I got up, made a half-pot of coffee, then went back into the living room and sat down to wait for it to perk. Or cook. Or whatever it is that coffee does to turn itself into a hot, delicious drink.

While I was sitting there, trying to decide how many cupcakes I was going to eat, the phone on the coffee table in front of me rang. Not my phone – wrong ringtone. A couple of bars of *New York State of Mind*. It was Tony's.

I ignored it and after a half-dozen rings it stopped. Then it rang again, eliciting the same response from me. I was a little surprised that his phone still worked, that he hadn't had it canceled or turned off or whatever it is you do when someone steals your phone.

The coffee pot dinged, signaling it was ... finished, so I made myself a cup, grabbed the cupcakes and went back into the living room, intending to enjoy a peaceful, healthy breakfast. But then the phone rang again. Probably Tony's wife, was my guess. Maybe that redhead whose picture was in his wallet. I decided to have a little fun and just before the last ring, I grabbed the phone and said, "Hello," in the sexiest voice I could manage at ten-fifteen in the morning.

"You fucking cunt! I'm going to kill you!"

Whoops. That wasn't what I was expecting to hear. Either Tony's wife had a *really* deep voice and a nasty vocabulary, or this was the man, himself – Tony! I looked at the phone. Yeah, a local number.

"What's up, Tony? How's the head?" I was feeling pretty cocky, knowing he didn't have a clue as to where I was.

"I'm gonna cut you up into little pieces while you're still alive and then I'm gonna take you out in a boat and feed the pieces to the sharks!"

That sent a shiver up my spine, but I said, "Ooh, is that how you do it in New York?"

"What? New York? I'm from California."

Whoops, again. "What do you want, Tony?" I said.

"I want my fucking shit back! All of it! Today!"

"Ain't gonna happen."

"You fucking cunt!"

"Yeah, you said that, already. Anything else?"

"WHERE'S MY STUFF?!!" he screamed at me.

"I'm sorry, I couldn't hear you. Could you repeat that?"

Silence from Tony's end.

"I threw it all away," I said.

"What? You didn't."

"Yeah, I did. In the garbage. It's gone."

"The money, too?"

I laughed. "No, I took that out of your wallet and kept it. I suppose you know it's counterfeit, don't you?"

"Not *that* money, you cunt! The fucking hundred and twenty grand!"

Cunt seemed to be Tony's choice of words when referencing that particular part of the female anatomy in a derogatory fashion. I hoped he didn't think he was insulting me. "What hundred and twenty grand?" I said. "All I took was two-forty."

"It was under the bed. In a tote bag."

"Oh, so that's what was in those two reams of paper?"

"They're not reams of paper – they're boxes of money. Sixty grand in each box."

"I've still got those. But the money's fake, right?"

A pause on Tony's end, then, "Yeah. Fake twenties. And if you don't give it back to me, they're gonna kill me."

"Who's gonna kill you?"

"Never mind who. So you still got it?"

"Yeah."

"I want it back. I don't give a shit about the rest of it – the clothes and stuff – but I want the money back. All of it. The $240, too."

I decided not to tell him about the two bills I'd attempted to put into circulation a little while earlier. "What's in it it for me?"

"I'll let you live."

I laughed. "Ooh, now that's a deal. That's your best offer?"

"Look, the money's no good to you. It's counterfeit. If you try to spend any of it, you could end up in prison for the rest of your life. Give it back to me and I'll be on my way and we'll just forget what happened between us yesterday. Okay?"

I considered his offer, not believing for a second that Tony would just forgive and forget. He wasn't the type. He was right about one thing, though – the money was no good to me. "Let me think about that, " I said. "I'll call you back."

"Wait! Don't hang up! You better give me back my money, cunt! If you don't, I'll –"

"Yeah, yeah, I know. Pieces and sharks." I hung up on him and turned off his phone.

Chapter 9

Three days later I was so horny I could hardly stand it. Julien still hadn't returned from his neighbor island sex sojourn, and my misadventure with Tony at the hotel had done absolutely zero to relieve my desire for a nice, stiff dick in my mouth. I was getting desperate, and they say that desperation can make a person take dangerous chances.

I'd checked the contents of the packages I thought were reams of paper and, just as claimed, inside was a hundred and twenty grand – sixty thousand bucks worth of fake money in each box. Poor Tony, losing all that money – I'll bet his partners were pissed. Maybe he was even dead by now, killed by them when he couldn't produce the missing bills. There hadn't been anything about a tourist getting murdered in Waikiki on the news lately, but that didn't really mean anything. There were lots of ways to get rid of a body in Hawaii. Like chopping it into pieces and feeding it to sharks.

He probably just ran away, back to the mainland. That's what I'd do if I knew someone was coming to kill me. Why stick around and make it easy for them? Of course, getting to the mainland without any *real* money, or clothes, or identification – especially identification – was difficult, if not impossible. So maybe Tony was, as the expression goes, *swimming with the fishes.*

Either way – dead or gone into hiding somewhere – Tony was no longer a problem for me so I decided it was time for another bus ride. I got dressed, stuffed some *real* money into my pocket – I never carry my wallet or phone or any ID when I go bus cruising – and made my way over to Kuhio Avenue to catch a bus.

Honolulu has perhaps the best bus system in the U.S. Hundreds and hundreds of buses cruise through Waikiki, the Ala Moana district, and downtown every day, heading to all parts of the island, and you seldom have to wait longer than five or ten minutes until one comes along going in your direction. Many of them are crowded, though. I like to catch one that's relatively empty, no matter what its destination.

I waited until one came along that was less than a quarter full, hopped on board and bought a day pass from the driver, then strolled down the aisle toward the back, checking out the passengers as I walked by. Nothing really interesting presented itself so I took a seat near the back and gazed out the window at the tourists as they wandered up and down the sidewalks of beautiful Waikiki. Lost in thought, I didn't notice Tony get on the bus until he sat down beside me and pressed a small knife against my side.

"Hey, bitch, what's up?"

Slightly in shock at seeing him still alive and sitting next to me, I mumbled an appropriate response. "Hey, Tony. Howzit?"

"I'm gonna fuck you up big time, cunt. I want my money!" He jabbed me lightly in the ribs with the tip of his knife, probably just to make sure I knew it was there.

I looked down at the knife. It wasn't very big. "That's kind of a small knife," I told him. A little voice inside my head said, *Don't be a wise ass – this is serious. You could get hurt. Or worse.* For some reason, though, I didn't feel as frightened as I should have, considering the situation I was in. Maybe it was because I considered Tony to be something of a dimwit and not very good at his job. After all, he lost 120 grand and all his possessions *and* he got beaten unconscious by a girl he met on a bus.

Tony grinned at me, although he didn't really seem to be in that great a mood. "It's not like a dick, sweetie. A two-inch blade can do a lot of damage."

The bus came to a stop and a swarm of tourists climbed aboard, crowding around the driver, buying day passes and asking questions. "C'mon, let's go," Tony said.

"Where?"

"Never mind where. Get your ass out of the seat and let's go!" He pulled me to my feet, pushing me toward the rear exit.

Since no one else had exited the bus, the rear doors were still closed. Tony yelled, "DOORS!" to the driver and I hopped down one step, preparing to get off when the doors opened. Tony grabbed me by the arm and yanked me back up to his level.

"What's your hurry?" he said. The knife was still in his hand and he held it flat against my back. Its small size made it hard for anyone else on the bus to see what was happening.

"Sorry. Just gonna get off the bus, is all."

"What? You think I'm stupid? I'm gonna let you go first? So you can run away?"

"I wasn't gonna run away," I lied. "And if you're so worried about it, you go first."

"Damn right I will. You better not fuck with me, bitch, or I'll stick this knife in your kidney."

I resisted a sudden urge to say, "Which one?" and instead said, "Okay, okay, I'll be good. Go ahead. You first."

The doors opened and Tony stepped down one step, leaving him a foot below me and directly in front. As he put his right foot forward to take the next step down, I planted *my* right foot into his upper back as hard as I could, sending him sprawling toward the sidewalk below. I hadn't really intended to do anything that dramatic and courageous but, considering the alternative – taking a walk somewhere with Tony and probably getting an unwanted lesson in how to carve human flesh – it was one of those things that fell under the heading, *it seemed like a good idea at the time.*

And it *was* a good idea. Tony went flying forward, dropping the knife onto the steps and throwing both arms out in front of him as he headed for the sidewalk, face first. Unfortunately for him, he was a bit late in getting those arms into a good landing position and his face hit the pavement just a few milliseconds before his hands.

I picked up the knife – a small lock-blade about two and a half inches long – and closed it, putting it in my pocket. Below me, on the sidewalk, a crowd had gathered around the bloodied and apparently unconscious Tony, alternately staring down at him and gazing up at me. I decided to wait until the next stop to get off and went back to my seat as the doors closed and the bus pulled away. For the first time, I noticed my heart was pounding in my chest. Several deep breaths and calming thoughts helped me to slow it down to a nearly-normal rhythm.

So, evidently Tony wasn't dead. Too bad, in my opinion. But this whole deal with the counterfeit money was getting completely out of hand, getting way too dangerous. There was no doubt in my mind that he'd been planning to use that little knife to cause me some pain. And while I might be okay with lots of things considered 'weird' by some people, pain was not one of them.

Chapter 10

Somewhat shaken by my encounter with Tony, I caught the next bus going in the opposite direction and went home. The horniness I'd felt earlier was gone, apparently frightened away by what had happened. Hopefully, that would turn out to be just a temporary condition.

I spent most of the day pondering my situation. Obviously, my problem was being caused by the money – the *fake* money – I took. Stole, technically. Of course, I didn't know what it was when I took it. I thought it was paper. If I'd known, well, ... I probably still would have taken it. Hell, it was a hundred and twenty grand and at the time I didn't know it was fake.

So, if taking the money caused my problem, giving it back should fix it. Maybe. There was always the possibility that Tony was the vindictive type and might still try to punish me in some way for all the complications I'd introduced into his plans for the phony money, whatever those plans had been. That subject had never come up in my conversations with my recently-acquired counterfeiter friend. After giving some more thought to what I should do, I realized what I really needed was a scheme that would remove Tony from my life for good and leave me free to pursue my bus-riding hobby in Waikiki.

Short of killing him – which I never *seriously* considered – I couldn't think of anything that would guarantee he'd leave me alone, even if I did return his money. However, I must confess that a few choice methods of permanently eliminating a person *did* occur to me. I especially liked the one Tony had mentioned earlier, the one involving sharks.

At a little past six I turned on the evening news and was surprised to see Tony staring back at me. Not him, actually – just some video of when he was being released from Queen's Hospital, earlier in the day, according to the female co-anchor. He'd been taken there for treatment of injuries suffered in a fall from a bus in Waikiki, she said.

Tony did not appear to be in great shape. His nose and forehead were bandaged and he had two shiners, both so big and black they looked liked truck tires surrounding his eyes, even though he was trying to hide them with sunglasses. It appeared his face-plant on the sidewalk had broken his nose.

"This is so sad," the female announcer was saying to her co-anchor, an older male named Horace. Horace Kelmore. I knew his name because he was the reason I watched this channel – I considered him to be a near-perfect dork!

"Yes, it is," he replied, nodding his agreement.

"A young man comes here for a vacation, and then, this."

"Yes, it's absolutely tragic. This is really an extremely unlucky individual. And there's more to the story, Jane."

Jane? I'd always thought that female announcer's name was Jennifer, or Jessica – something like that. Whatever.

"More bad luck? What else?" Jane said.

"Well, I spoke to some of my sources at the hotel where he's staying, and they told me that the hotel is comping his room."

"You mean, he's getting his hotel room for free?" Jane sounded absolutely astounded. I briefly wondered if these two had rehearsed this overly-dramatic shtick they were presenting or if it was completely ad-lib.

"Yes, totally free."

"That doesn't sound like bad luck to me, Horace," Jane said. "Free is good."

"Not always, Jane. It's the reason he's getting the room at no charge that makes it bad. Shortly after he arrived here on vacation, he was attacked in his hotel room by an unknown individual and beaten unconscious."

"Oh, no!"

"Yes. And that's not all. This individual then proceeded to rob the young man of all his possessions."

"That's a terrible, terrible story, Horace. Thank you for sharing it with us."

Hmm, that was interesting. Was she being sincere or sarcastic? Hard to tell.

"I also interviewed a young lady, a tourist who was waiting for another bus and saw the whole thing happen," Horace continued.

"Really? And?"

"She said he apparently lost his balance as he was stepping down – we all know those bus steps are steep, Jane – and he came flying out of the bus and landed face-first on the pavement."

"Ouch," Jane said.

"Yeah, ouch. She said there was a young woman standing behind him, also waiting to get off the bus, and she was so shocked by what happened that all she could do was return to her seat and sit back down."

"I'll bet. Indeed, shocking. Thank you, Horace, for bringing us up to date on this story." Jane turned away from her co-anchor and back toward the camera. "Another sad story wraps up our look at local news. At least he's getting his room for free. I suppose that's something." She paused briefly, then said, "Malik will be here with sports when we return, right after this commercial break, so stay tuned." She smiled into the camera and continued smiling until she was replaced by an ad for used cars.

Wow, what a story. They never identified Tony by name and they never identified the shocked young woman who was standing behind him on the bus. Since that young woman was me, I was especially pleased with that part of Horace's report. Apparently, everyone thought what happened to Tony was an accident, and he wasn't disputing that version of events.

I turned off the TV and sat there, thinking. For some strange reason, the story about Tony's fall had given me an idea – a scheme to get rid of him, more or less permanently, without actually murdering him. It would involve a little bit of work to accomplish but, if it removed that asshole from my life, it would be well worth it. Plus, it seemed like it would also be fun. Horrible, evil fun, my favorite kind!

Step number one of my plan involved contacting Tony and telling him I wanted to give back the money. So that's what I did. Using his phone, I called him back at the number he'd called me from. That turned out to be the front desk of the hotel. A friendly female voice connected me to his room.

The phone rang several times before a groggy-sounding Tony answered. "Waff if it?" he mumbled. Apparently I'd interrupted a late-afternoon nap. Those pain pills they give you when you plant your face into a sidewalk can make you really sleepy, I've heard.

I hummed a few bars of *New York State of Mind* into the phone.

"Hew fuffin coont," was Tony's fuzzy-sounding response to my greeting, which probably wouldn't have made much sense to most people, but I knew what he meant. It wasn't really much of an insult, to my way of thinking.

"How come you sound so funny?" I said.

"Hew froke my fuffin jaw, coont! Iff wiyud shuff."

That was a surprise – they hadn't mentioned that on the news. "Broken, huh? Maybe you shouldn't threaten people with a knife," I told him.

"Fuffin coont!"

"Yeah, yeah. Listen, Tony, I've decided to give you your money back."

"Waff?"

"Tomorrow afternoon. Three o'clock. Your hotel room. I'll have a delivery service bring it. With instructions not to leave it if you aren't there."

"I neev it fuday," he said.

"Not a chance. Tomorrow, three o'clock. If you want your money back, be there." I hung up before he could call me a cunt again. A smile spread over my face as I made a mental check mark next to step one of my plan. Tony was about to become much less of a problem for little old me!

Chapter 11

Step two of my plan involved the police. I called them, again using Tony's phone, and eventually ended up speaking to a sympathetic female officer who identified herself as Lisa. Not Officer Lisa – just Lisa. I told her my name was Barbara.

"So, what seems to be the problem, Barbara?" she said, after our brief introductions.

"Well, ..." I began, deliberately trying to sound hesitant.

"It's all right, Barbara. Take your time."

"Well, it's ..."

"Is this about a domestic situation? About your husband, perhaps? Or boyfriend?"

"Well, ... sort of." Still hesitant. I wanted Lisa to drag the details out of me.

"Is he ... mistreating you?"

"Oh, no. Tony's a great guy," I said.

"I see. So, then, what seems to be the problem?"

"I'm afraid."

"Of this person, Tony?"

"No, no. I'm not afraid of Tony. He wouldn't hurt me. He loves me."

"Just who is this Tony, anyway? Is he your husband?"

"He's my boyfriend. Sort of. I just met him a few days ago, but we clicked right away, you know. He's from California, just visiting." I could hear the keys of her computer clacking away as she typed up the lies I was telling her about me and Tony.

"All right," Lisa said. "He's your boyfriend, recently acquired. And what? You're having some kind of problem with him?"

"Yeah. Well, not with him, exactly. With these friends of his. Tony's a really sweet guy. He wouldn't hurt a fly." *Yeah, right!* said that little voice inside my head.

"So it's his friends that you're afraid of?"

"Yeah. They're a nasty bunch."

"What, exactly, is it that you're afraid of?" Lisa said.

"I'm worried these so-called friends of his are going to get Tony into trouble. Big trouble. Maybe even dead. Or in jail."

Lisa's interest in my story seemed to suddenly perk up. "Really, Barbara? And how would they do that?"

"Well, they're ..." I paused for dramatic effect. "... counterfeiters."

Lisa returned my pause, though I suspected hers was a pause of confusion, not for effect. At last she said, "I'm sorry. Could you say that again?"

"They're counterfeiters. And they're gonna get Tony in trouble, I know it. I just know it." I added a couple of fake sobs at the end, to let Lisa know how *truly* concerned I was about Tony's welfare.

"I see. Counterfeiters." The keys to her computer were clacking up a storm in the background. "And how is your boyfriend involved in all this?"

"They've talked him into helping them pass the bills."

"Bills?"

"Yeah. Fake twenty dollar bills. Hundreds of thousands of dollars worth. There's this group of guys, see. And starting Friday night, as soon as all the banks are closed, they're going to start spending these bills all over the island. You know, buy some item that costs a buck, pay for it with a fake twenty and get nineteen real dollars in change."

"Yes, I know how it works," Lisa said. "And your boyfriend, Tony, is a member of this group, this gang of counterfeiters?"

"No, no, he's not a member. Not yet, anyway. That's why I called you guys. The police, I mean. I want you to stop him before he gets involved in, ... in this plan to distribute all this fake money."

"I see."

It was time to set the hook, I decided. "Tomorrow afternoon, all these guys are supposed to have a meeting in Tony's hotel room and some guy is gonna show up with the money and give it to them so they can divide it up and get ready to pass it this weekend."

Clack, clack, clack. That really was a noisy keyboard. "Uh-huh. Go on," said Lisa.

"I was thinking maybe your people – the police, I mean – could show up and arrest these guys before Tony gets involved, you know. He hasn't done anything, yet. All he's done is listen to their plans and, well, *sort of* agreed to help them."

"And all this is about a counterfeiting scheme. Right?"

"Yeah. About passing counterfeit money. So, can you help? I *really* don't want Tony to get into trouble. Can you do something?"

"I'm sure we can," Lisa said. "Counterfeiting's a serious crime, and we'd certainly like to stop these people before they put a large amount of phony bills into circulation."

"That's great."

"And the meeting's tomorrow, you say?"

"Yeah, tomorrow." I gave her the rest of the information about the supposed meeting – Tony's hotel and room number and the time of the meeting – and then waited while she typed it up.

"All right," she said at last. "Now just let me get a little more information about you, Barbara, starting with your full name."

"Uh, ... I don't think I want to get more involved than I already am," I said, then hung up and switched off the phone before Lisa could ask any additional questions about me.

So. That took care of step number two in what I had come to think of as my *diabolical master plan*. Only one more step to take care of and I could sit back and watch everything unfold, automatically, without me having to do anything else. But the next step was the most difficult step of all.

Step number three involved me going back down to Kalakaua Avenue and convincing a guy I didn't even know to help me with my plan. His name was Wally the Weed Guy and he worked the sidewalk up near International Market Place, selling weed to tourists. That wasn't his real name, of course, but all the locals – even the cops – knew who he was and that's what they called him. The cops mostly ignored him. Policing in Waikiki is about keeping the tourists happy, after all. And scoring a little local bud, even though it was still illegal in Hawaii, seemed to be high – no pun intended – on many visitors' *to do* lists.

I changed clothes and got ready to leave, taking three hundred dollars in counterfeit money out of one of the boxes and stuffing the bills into my pocket. With Tony temporarily on the disabled list, I wasn't worried about bumping into him. All I needed to do now was find Wally and persuade him to go along with my scheme. That probably wasn't going to be a problem, I figured. I had ways of convincing guys to help me out, if you know what I mean.

Chapter 12

Wally the Weed Guy was in his usual spot by the Marketplace, hawking his wares to the tourists. I watched him for a while. Most of his customers seemed to be visitors from Asia. That made sense, I guess. Some of those Asian tourists came from countries where getting caught with a little weed meant 15 or 20 years in prison, and they probably just wanted to see what the big deal was.

When there was a break in his traffic, I approached him.

"Hey, sweetie, looking to score?" He smiled at me from a face almost completely obscured by a giant, tangled mess of facial hair – his beard and mustache – and long, sun-bleached, brown hair. A gaudy blue aloha shirt and a puka-shell necklace added to the illusion he was a time traveler, a hippy, visiting from the San Francisco of the 1960s.

"Not exactly," I told him.

He frowned and his eyes scanned the sidewalk, apparently seeking out potential future customers who *were* looking to score a little weed. "So whaddaya want?"

"You got time for a little chat?"

"Time's money, sweetie. Make it quick."

"Actually, this is about money. It's a ..." I paused, searching for the right words to describe what I wanted Wally to do. "... business proposition. A one-time deal. Take you about a half-hour and there's 300 bucks in it for you."

"Okay, what's the catch? This is something illegal, right?"

"No, it's not. It's just, well, it's kinda complicated, but I met this guy who's visiting from the mainland and we shacked up for a week or so, and ... uh, I ended up with some of his stuff and now he's leaving and I want to give him his stuff back and I need someone to do it for me. I don't want to do it myself because, ... well, I just don't want to see him again."

"Yeah? So what, you stole this stuff from him?"

"Fuck, no! I didn't steal it. He just left it at my place."

"Three hundred bucks, huh? That seems like a lot for a half-hour's work. Is he violent or something?"

"No. Not at all. He's a sweetheart. But like I said, I just don't want to see him. He's leaving. It's over between us."

Wally paused, as if he was giving my proposition serious thought, then said, "Nah, I don't think I want to do it. I make plenty of money, right here, selling weed."

What? Shit! That's not what he was supposed to say. I expected him to say something like, "Why, sure, little missy! Ah'd be plumb happy to help you out. A feller can always use an extra 300 clams!" Or something like that. Although I have absolutely no idea at all why I imagined he'd say it in a hillbilly drawl.

"Am I hearing this correctly?" I said. "You're turning down 300 bucks for less than an hour's work? I'll bet you don't make that much money selling weed."

"Sometimes I do," he said with a smirky grin.

"Really? Profit? Three hundred dollars profit?"

The grin vanished. "No. Not profit."

"So?"

"I'm just not feeling it, ya know? I'd like to help you out but something about the deal doesn't quite seem legit."

"But it is," I protested.

"Yeah, well, ..."

I could sense Wally was torn between wanting to make a quick buck and worry over the legitimacy of *the deal.* Couldn't blame him for worrying, I suppose – I probably should have taken more time and come up with a better story. Whatever. Guys are easy. Practically any girl can sweet-talk just about any guy into doing what she wants. And for those rare times when sweet-talk wasn't working, a girl could always sweeten *the deal*, itself. I decided that perhaps it was time for me to sweeten *the deal* for Wally the Weed Guy.

A brief look up and down the sidewalk satisfied me no one was paying any attention to Wally and me as we stood there, out of the flow of foot traffic, talking. I stepped forward until I was practically leaning on him, so that it looked as if I was whispering a secret into his ear. Then, with my right hand, I reached down and grabbed his junk through his shorts, giving it a couple of light squeezes before stepping back. "Are you sure I can't convince you to change your mind?" I said, smiling at him.

Wally grinned at me out of that mass of facial hair. Nice, straight, white teeth – at least, what I could see of them. "Yeah, maybe. Maybe I *could* help you out."

"Great. You live around here?"

"Hawaii Kai," he said.

Well, shit! Another setback. Hawaii Kai was miles from here, out on the eastern end of the island, and even at this time – it was almost eight at night – Kalaniana'ole Highway would be packed with cars, making the drive take well over an hour. That ruled out a trip to Wally's place. I didn't want to get stuck out in Hawaii Kai and have to spend the night with him because he was too tired to bring me back to Waikiki.

"How do you get to work?" I asked him.

"Car. I drive to work."

"Where's your car?"

"Seaside Avenue. There's an underground parking garage up there. I park there."

Seaside was the next side street back up Kalakaua, if you didn't count Duke's Lane, which was basically just an alley. "How's the lighting in that garage?" I said.

"It's okay, I guess. Kinda on the dim side, maybe."

"Perfect." I grabbed him by the hand and before he could protest or say anything at all, we were heading up the sidewalk toward Seaside Avenue. "I can't wait to see this car of yours," I told him. "I hope it has a comfortable back seat."

Chapter 13

Wally's car was an old clunker, so dirty I couldn't tell what company had made it. Most of it was a dull charcoal color, except for the right front fender, which was lime green. I didn't bother to ask why.

Evidently Wally spent much of his life in this car. The front seat area was littered with fast food wrappers, plastic cups and straws, and a variety of well-worn magazines. "Sorry about the mess," he said as he unlocked it. "I wasn't expecting company, ya know."

"Don't worry about it," I said.

"It's not fancy but it drives good. Very dependable. You wanna go somewhere?"

"Yeah, the back seat."

"Sounds good to me," he said.

We climbed into the back seat. Compared to the front of his car, this area was pristine. It appeared as if no one had ever sat back here.

The car was parked in an ideal location for what I had in mind. It was at the far end of the garage and what Wally had described as 'dim' light was closer to no light at all. Pretty fucking dark would have been a more accurate description. In other words, perfect.

"Take off your pants," I told him.

"What are you gonna do?"

I gave him my best *what, are you stupid?* look and said, "Whaddaya think I'm gonna do, Wally? I'm gonna give you a prostate exam."

He giggled and pulled down his pants, saying, "I hope you're just kidding."

His cock was already at half-mast, kinda just wobbling around as it struggled to stand upright. I wrapped my hand around it and began lightly squeezing it in a rhythmic fashion. Almost immediately it sprang to attention. He responded with a long, moaning, drawn-out, "Ooooohhh," as I continued to massage it.

"Nice dick," I said. It *was* nice – good length, full-bodied, clean and tasty-looking.

"Thanks. I like it."

I began sliding my hand up and down his shaft, slowly and gently, while I gazed down at him and tried to look sexy. Although I'm not sure he could even see my face – this corner of the garage was *really* poorly illuminated.

"Lemme see your pussy," he said.

"Nope."

"No?"

"Tomorrow. After you help me out of that little problem with my boyfriend, we'll go somewhere and I'll show it to you. You can fuck it and eat it – do whatever you want to." I threw in a couple of extra-friendly tugs as I fondled his dick, which already was as hard as that statue I'd used to conk Tony in the head.

"So what is this, then? A preview? You're just gonna jerk me off today?"

"Better than that, Wally. I'm gonna suck that little monster dry." I leaned forward and planted a long, slow tongue-slide on the bottom of his cock, running it all the way up from his balls to the head and then exiting with a couple of slurpy swirls around the tip, including a loud smacking sound for emphasis. "Kinda like that," I added as I sat back up.

"Ohhhh, fuck!" was Wally's reaction. "Don't stop now. I love having my dick sucked by a beautiful babe."

Ooh, he called me beautiful. That's gonna be worth a couple of extra licks around the head of his dick when he cums. I wiggled myself into a comfortable position between Wally's legs and pulled his dick up to my mouth, not putting it in but just rubbing the head lightly back and forth across my lips.

"Oh, fuck, fuck, fuck! That feels soooo good!"

I parted my lips and scarfed up about a half-inch of his cockhead, massaging the tip with my tongue. He seemed to like that. Or, at least, his dick did. It began dancing around in my mouth.

"Ohhhh, nooooo," was his vocal reaction, followed by a warning, "Fuck, I'm gonna cum!"

That was quick. *Really* quick. Apparently Wally hadn't had his dick drained recently. Well, I didn't want to mess up his pristine back seat by letting him shoot a load all over it – and maybe all over me, too – so I chose the best option available. I gobbled his cock into my mouth and sucked, just as he let loose with a massive blast of thick, warm jizz.

"Oh, shit! Fuck! I'm sorry. I couldn't wait!" he said.

I wanted to tell him not to worry about it, it was all right, but it's kinda hard to carry on a conversation when your mouth's full of cum and dick. So I just mumbled, "ummmm," swallowed the load and continued munching on that rapidly-shrinking cock while Wally jerked and twitched and went, "Oh, oh, oh!" every time my tongue *accidentally* swiped over his dickhead. When his dick had shrunk to less than half its hard-on size and was no longer reacting to my tongue, I released it and got to my knees.

"I'm sorry," he said again.

"Don't worry about it," I told him. "Tomorrow will be better. *Much* better. No need to apologize." Which was true. I wasn't upset that Wally had just cum in world-record time, that he wasn't able to hold his load. It didn't really matter to me. I wasn't doing this for fun. This was a business blowjob – no humming included.

"So, I'll see you again, tomorrow?"

"Absolutely. There's two small boxes of stuff I want you to return to Tony. That's my ex. I told him to be in his hotel room at three o'clock if he wanted his things back, so I'll come by and give them to you a few minutes before that. His hotel's just up the street from here, just past Kuhio."

"Up this street?" he said, pointing at the front of the garage. "Seaside?"

"Yeah. So this whole thing should probably take only 15 or 20 minutes."

"Okay. And then what?"

"I'll wait for you here, by the garage, and then we'll go somewhere. Maybe to my place – I live nearby. In Kaimuki."

"Sounds good."

"It's gonna be better than good," I said, giving his limp dick a final squeeze as I prepared to leave. "It's gonna be spec-fucking-tacular!"

"Hey, what about the money?" he said, as I opened the car door.

"Money?" I hadn't told Wally he'd be delivering money? How did he know about that?

"Yeah, the 300 bucks. You said you'd give me half up front."

Oh, that money! I'd forgotten about that. I closed the door and dug the fake twenties out of my pocket, fanning them out in front of Wally's face for him to see. Then I ripped them in half and handed the 15 half-pieces to him, putting the other 15 halves back in my pocket. "Half up front," I said.

"What the fuck? What am I supposed to do with this?"

"Wait 'til tomorrow and I'll give you the rest, the other half."

"And then what?"

"I don't know. Take them to the bank and deposit them. Or swap them for new bills. Up to you."

"The bank's gonna ask me what happened to the money. Why it's ripped in half. I think that's against the law – destroying money."

"Tell them your girlfriend got pissed off at you and did it."

"Then they're gonna ask me her name, where she lives, all that shit."

"Well, make something up. Tell them you only just met her, her name was Sharon something – you never learned her last name – and right after she ripped up your money, she got on a plane and went back to the mainland." And then I added something that may or may not have been true. I really had no idea. "And don't worry about it so much. They have to swap the money for you. It's a federal law. If you come in with damaged money, even if it's in two pieces, the law says they have to replace it for you."

"Good to know," Wally said.

I opened the car door and got out. "You coming?" I said.

"I already came. I think I'll just stay here and rest for a while." With it being so dark, I couldn't tell if he was grinning or not when he said that, but I suspect he was.

"Yeah, right. Okay, I'll see you tomorrow, about quarter to three. By the Marketplace."

"I'll be there," he said.

I closed the car door and left the parking garage, walking up Seaside to Kuhio Avenue and then down Kuhio toward Diamond Head and home. It was a beautiful evening, warm but with a cooling breeze as the trade winds swept down across the Ko'olau Mountains. Chattering tourists filled the sidewalks as I strolled along, a smile on my lips and the lingering taste of cum in my mouth. One more day to go and no more problems with Tony!

The three parts of my *master plan* had been activated. All I had to do now was deliver the counterfeit money to Wally and let him take it to Tony. The cops would take care of the rest!

Chapter 14

At ten to three the next day, I met up with Wally in front of International Market Place, carrying Tony's tote bag with the two boxes of fake twenties inside. He was wearing the exact-same clothes as yesterday. I briefly wondered if he fell asleep in his car after I left and ended up spending the night there.

"That the stuff?" he said, nodding in the direction of the bag.

"Yeah. C'mon, let's go." I led the way, heading up Kalakaua toward Seaside Avenue.

"What's in these boxes, anyway?" he said, looking into the bag.

"Oh, a bunch of photos, a belt, small stuff, like that."

"How big is this guy, anyway?"

"Tony? He's not that big. Why? You worried he's gonna punch you out or something?"

"Yeah, well, the thought crossed my mind, you know. I don't wanna get beat up and have to miss work. Somebody might steal my spot."

"That's not gonna happen. I guarantee it."

"No?"

"No. You heard about that guy that fell off the bus yesterday?"

"Sure. What a klutz!"

"That's him."

"Who?"

"Tony, my ex. He's all banged up. Two black eyes, a seriously-broken nose, and a broken jaw. He's definitely not going to start a fight with you."

"Good to know," Wally said. "So, what happened, anyway?"

"Whaddaya mean?"

"How did he fall off the bus?"

"Oh, that. When I talked to him on the phone, he said someone pushed him as he was getting off."

"No shit!"

"That's what he said."

"Fuck, Waikiki's getting to be a dangerous place," Wally observed.

We came to Seaside and turned, heading up toward Kuhio Avenue. When we got to the parking garage, he said, "You gonna wait here for me?"

"I think I'm gonna wait up there," I said, pointing up the street. "There's some benches up there. I'll just sit there and wait and then pick you up when you come back down the street. Okay?"

"Sure."

We said goodbye when we got to Kuhio. I found a seat on one of the concrete benches and watched as Wally crossed the street and continued up Seaside. The hotel was only a hundred yards or so up the street, on the left side, so from where I was sitting I had an excellent view of the front. Like many hotels in Waikiki, there were no front doors – just a big, wide lobby that opened directly out onto the sidewalk. Go up five or six steps and there you were, inside the hotel.

I watched as Wally started up those steps. He made it about halfway and then stopped as two uniformed police officers appeared at the top of the steps, blocking his path. That removed a major worry from my mind – I'd been concerned the cops wouldn't show.

The two cops had a few words with Wally and then the three of them disappeared into the lobby. I was pretty sure I knew what was going to happen next – the cops would arrest Wally and then another cop, obviously dressed in civilian clothes, would deliver the counterfeit bills to Tony's room. Once he accepted the money from the cop, it would be the end of the line for old buttfucker Tony. Although, maybe he'd get into that activity once he got settled in prison. A girl can dream, can't she?

I wished I could be there – could see what was happening. Of course, that was out of the question. Too dangerous. I'd have to wait until the cops brought Tony out and put him in one of the police cars that were just now pulling out of hidden driveways and parking spaces and converging on the hotel.

I felt reasonably secure down here on Kuhio, 100 yards away, though. That was because Seaside Avenue was a one-way street, heading away from Kuhio, up toward Ala Wai Boulevard. So when the cops left, presumably with Tony handcuffed in the back seat of one of the patrol cars, they'd be heading away from my position.

It was a long wait. I began to get nervous. What the fuck was taking so long? Did something go wrong?

I stood up and got ready to leave. If something had gone wrong, it probably wasn't a good idea for me to be in the nearby vicinity. And then, as I took one last look at the hotel, two cops appeared at the entrance to the hotel, walked down the steps, got into their cars and drove away.

Two more cops appeared at the top of the hotel steps, and then a shitload of them, most in uniform but a few in civilian clothes, as well. FBI, maybe? Counterfeiting was a federal crime, after all.

And finally, the *big show!* What I'd been waiting for. Out came Tony, in handcuffs, flanked by two men in business suits. More FBI, probably. He was too far away for me to see the expression on his face, but I could imagine what he was saying to himself – first, "Fuffin' copf." And then, "Vat fuffin' coont. I'b gonna kig her."

Yeah, right, Tony. You're gonna kill me. Maybe in about 30 years, when you get out of prison. If you can find me!

And, then right behind them, also handcuffed and flanked by two suits, came Wally. *Bummer, Wally. Looks like that big sex adventure you had planned for today ain't gonna happen.* No need for him to panic, though. I was sure that once he told the cops his story about how a beautiful young woman gave him a blowjob and 300 bucks to deliver a package, they'd realize he'd been set up and release him.

Yeah, right! said that little voice inside my head, making me smile.

It was starting to get dark – the sun sets early in Honolulu – but I stayed and watched until all the cops had left, their cars moving, parade-like, up to the corner of Ala Wai Boulevard, where they turned left and disappeared. To tell you the truth, Tony's arrest had been a lot less satisfying than what I'd anticipated. I thought I'd get more of a thrill out of seeing him carted away in cuffs, but that's not what I was feeling. What I was really experiencing was disappointment.

Oh, sure, I was glad Tony was out of my life – hopefully, forever. But I was left with a sort-of unsatisfied feeling. I was disappointed. Disappointed and horny. That blowjob I'd given Wally the day before had done absolutely nothing for me, and I'd been horny since before Tony made his spectacular exit from the bus. For me, that was a long time.

Well, I knew just the cure for that. I crossed the street, waited patiently until a bus came by and I hopped on. This time of day, the buses weren't usually that full. The area's day-shift workers had long departed and were now distributed around the island, probably watching TV with their families or having dinner. Many visitors were already in their hotel rooms, nursing sunburns or being just too tired from a day at the beach to go out. And the ones who did go out didn't seem to ride the bus – they apparently preferred to wander the streets, oohing and ahhing and taking hundreds of pictures of anything that looked as if it would be out of place in Ohio or Canada.

The bus I'd climbed aboard was no exception. Perhaps 10 people were scattered throughout, most of them gazing out the window. A couple of elderly women gave me a bored, disinterested look as I walked up the aisle. And then I saw him.

He was sitting there, almost at the back of the bus, reading a book. Or rather, *trying* to read a book. His eyes were closed and his head kept falling forward, threatening to dislodge his glasses from their perch halfway down his nose. And if I had to take a guess, I'd say he cut his own hair. In other words, my perfect man!

I sat down beside him, which woke him up. "Hi," I said, treating him to a flirty smile. "Mind if I sit next to you?"

He slid over to give me more room and smiled back at me. That was always a good sign. "Not at all," he said. "Not at all."

I smiled again. Inwardly, this time – to myself. Sometimes, a simple activity like riding the bus can be *so much fun !!*

the end – fini – owari

Hey! Get your hand out of your crotch! This story's over. But there are lots more of my stories about horny young men and juicy young women available at your favorite online bookstore. Check them out, and while you're at it, please leave a (hopefully favorable) review. If you do, I'll write more stories, just for you.

In the meantime, here's a sample from Book 2 of <u>The Waikiki Hummer</u> series, as well as samples from Book 1 of my ongoing <u>Pleasantly Plump</u> series and Book 1 of my ongoing <u>Mike and Melanie</u> series. Hope you like them.

Shannon

The Man from UAPIG
A Waikiki Hummer Adventure – Book 2 (Sample)

Chapter 1

I was reading about myself online last night. It was mostly a bunch of bullshit – speculation about who I really am, what I do and why I do it. Dozens of articles full of rumors, gossip, and third-hand accounts of supposed encounters made interesting reading for the bored masses, I suppose, even though most of it was complete nonsense. Of course, that's what you get on the internet.

One piece, however, got it more right than wrong, at least at the end. Called *The Waikiki Hummer – Who Is She?* the article summed it up like this:

And while we don't know her name or why she does it, there are a few things we <u>do</u> know about the Waikiki Hummer. She's young, an attractive blonde in her early twenties. She likes to ride the buses of Honolulu, picking up male tourists and accompanying them to their hotels. And she then proceeds to give them what most have described as, "the best blowjob of my life!"

She doesn't charge a fee and she doesn't take tips, so she's not a hooker. This appears to be her hobby or just something she does for fun. Oh, and there's a reason they call her the Hummer – she likes to hum as she performs oral sex. In fact, she even takes requests for favorite songs!

That pretty much perfectly described me and my 'hobby.' And it certainly described what was, at this very instant, happening in room 1123 of a well-known Waikiki hotel, nameless here for legal reasons.

His name was Marvin, he was a college professor from Austin and, just as described in the article, I met him on the bus. He was also, from my point of view, anyway, nearly perfect. A totally bald head was highlighted by a white visor with the word *Aloha* written across the bill, while thick eyeglasses perched halfway down his nose, magnifying his eyes and making them appear cartoonishly large in his pudgy face. This wonderfully dorky look was completed by an embroidered, western-style shirt and a string tie with a turquoise slide. I started getting wet the minute I spotted him, sitting there all alone in the back seat of the bus.

I know, I know. Not many 23-year-old girls are into dorky, middle-aged guys. I've wondered about it myself. Was I looking for a father figure, a daddy substitute, a guy who looked like my dad? Not likely – dear old dad is six feet, two inches tall and slender, with a full head of hair.

Whatever. Dorky – that's my type. I like what I like and I'm not ashamed of it.

Anyway, after convincing Marvin that he and I should spend some time in his hotel room, here we were, both of us naked and me with his dick in my mouth, humming *The Eyes of Texas* as I sucked on it. See? Just like in that article.

"How we doing up there?" I asked him, temporarily spitting out his dick but continuing to massage it with my hand. Marvin was lying on the bottom half of the bed, with his legs dangling over the end and his feet on the floor, and I was kneeling between his legs.

"Fufudool," came the muffled reply. The smothered sound of his reply was no doubt caused by the fact that his face was covered by a pillow – an effort to mute the squeals, shrieks, and screeches that emerged from his mouth each time I slurped my tongue across the head of his dick. My new friend, Marvin, was a screamer!

"Great," I said, although I had no idea what 'fufudool' meant. Maybe 'wonderful?' Whatever, I popped his cock back into my mouth and went back to work, sipping and sucking and slurping away.

Marvin had a very nice, very enjoyable dick. It was big, but not too big, Thick, but not too thick. Firm, but – well, let's just leave it at firm.

Very firm. It was what I like to call a Goldilocks cock – not too big, not too small, just right!

And he had great staying power, too. In my career as the Hummer, I'd gone through this same routine many times – picked up a dorky-looking, middle-aged guy and ended up in his hotel room with his cock in my mouth. Just like that article said. And almost always, the guy had rewarded me by splashing that first load of warm, delicious cum down my throat in less than a minute. I expected that and wasn't disappointed because I knew we were just getting started. By the time I was finished with them, most dicks had been in my mouth for a couple of hours and had cum multiple times.

Marvin, however, was different. I'd been working on his stiffy for at least 15 minutes and it was still as firm and erect as when we first started. I'd used my lips and my tongue and even a little bit of teeth-scraping on his dickhead, but my only reward had been him screaming and jerking and twitching so violently I thought he might bounce off the bed. I wasn't discouraged, though. If anything, his reluctance to gift me with my reward only made me more determined because I knew that when I finally did get my present, it was going to be a big one!

So I continued. I swirled my tongue around the head of his cock in a clockwise direction, then reversed and did the same in the opposite direction. Muffled moans and groans escaped from under his pillow and his body jerked around and bucked like a rodeo horse.

Pretending it was an ear of corn, I turned his dick sideways and nibbled back and forth along the shaft, tonguing the head every time I got to that end. He screamed into the pillow but Little Marvin stayed stubborn and firm.

I slurped his balls into my mouth and spent some time sucking on those while I continued to massage his dick with my hand. Still no dick-juice emerged to compensate me for my efforts. Marvin was, as a doctor might say, *a difficult case!*

"Everything still good, Marvin?" I asked him.

He removed the pillow from his face, lifted himself up onto his elbows and looked down at me. "Can you come up here? On the bed, with me?" he said.

"Sure." I clambered up onto the bed, next to him. "What can I do for you?"

He slid backwards so that his whole body was lying on the bed and his cock was sticking up in the air, staggering around like a drunk sailor. "Well, uh, ... I was wondering, ... uh, ..."

"It's okay," I told him, steadying his dick and milking it with my hand. "Tell me. Don't be shy."

"Can I ... can I ...?"

"Can you what, Marvin?"

"Taste your pussy. Can I taste your pussy?"

Hmm. Apparently old Marvin, here, wasn't as shy and inexperienced as I'd thought when I first saw him on the bus. Maybe that explained his unusual staying power. "You wanna eat my pussy?"

He nodded and smiled up at me. "Yeah, I do."

"Sounds like a winner." I released his cock, climbed up near the head of the bed and swung my leg up and over his head, planting my wet, juicy cunt directly onto his waiting mouth. "How's that, Marvin?" I said.

"Feewissis," he said, running his tongue up my slit and lapping up a mouthful of pussy juice. "Abfowooftwee feewissis!"

I rocked back and forth on his face for a while, enjoying his warm tongue as it slid back and forth, deeper and deeper into my pussy. I wasn't sure exactly how this was going to encourage Marvin to shoot his load, but it was worth a try. And it felt *great!*

Just when I began to think *I* might be the one to cum, he lifted me high off his face and said, very clearly this time, "Can you turn around?"

"Sixty-nine?" I said, looking down from my mid-air perch above him.

"Yeah. I like that."

"Excellent. Me, too. We can do that." I spun around and replanted my pussy onto his mouth, then leaned down and sucked his cock back into my mouth, concentrating on the head. That's the sensitive part, where all the nerve-ends are, you know. In the head. You can lick the shaft of a dick forever and it won't cum, but put some effort into slurping the head and you'll soon be rewarded. Yup, that's my advice – concentrate on the dickhead!

So that's what I did – I took my own advice. While Marvin stayed busy trying to devour my pussy, I concentrated on the head of his cock, lapping and licking and teasing it by dancing my tongue across it, causing it to jump around as if it was playing dodge-ball with my tongue. I felt both Marvin *and* his dick tense up and begin to spasm and I knew I had him – I was about to get my reward.

And get a reward I did! Marvin used both hands to pull my pussy wide open and buried his face in it, mumbling something that sounded like, "Fook, fook, fook, ooohhhhhhh, fook!" He then proceeded to unload a monstrous stream of rapid-fire spurts of warm, creamy cum onto my tongue, which was licking the underside of his dickhead. Not surprisingly, I struggled a bit with that – tonguing his dick and, at the same time, swallowing the massive amount of jizz with which he was gifting me. But, thanks to lots of previous practice, I managed to accomplish both successfully.

Actually, I love this part, where the guy cums in my mouth and as I swallow it all up and continue to suck, his dick gradually surrenders and shrinks in size. It makes me feel powerful, as if there had been a little battle between the guy's cock and my mouth, and my mouth had won, reducing that cock to a whimpering, withered shell of its former glory. I'm pretty sure if it weren't for the feeling of power that comes with draining a guy's dick, I'd have a completely different hobby. Tennis, maybe.

Anyway, after emptying Marvin's dick and reducing it in both size and stiffness, I continued sucking on it. That squirmy little bugger was all wet and slippery and super-sensitive, and it kept trying to run away and hide from my tongue, but it was spectacularly unsuccessful. Marvin had also stopped munching on my pussy. I could hear him back there, panting loudly and trying to catch his breath, so I released his dick from my mouth with a loud, smacking sound, turned around and joined him, laying my head next to his on his pillow.

After he'd caught his breath, he looked at me and smiled. "Oh, wow!" he said. "Fuck! Wow! That was amazing – the best ever! I've *never* had a blowjob that good. That'll last me for a month, at least!"

Oh, foolish, foolish Marvin, I thought. *A month? It's not even going to last you the rest of the afternoon. You'd better get comfortable, Marvin, 'cause we're just getting started!*

Chapter 2

Three hours later, Marvin's cock was no longer a functioning entity. Too bad. I'd really enjoyed Marvin, his pussy licking, and his tasty dick. And I'm pretty sure Marvin enjoyed me, too. At least, that was the impression I got as I was leaving. He was lying on the bed, naked, with his dick a total wreck and a stupid grin on his face. He didn't say anything – he just smiled and gave me a little three-finger wave goodbye as I closed the door.

That was fun. I even got off a couple of times, thanks to Marvin's long and enjoyable tongue. But, having destroyed his cock, it was time to get on home. Not even a dedicated cocksucker like me can suck dicks *all* day.

It was only eight or nine blocks back to my place, down at the Diamond Head end of Waikiki, so I walked home, zigzagging my way around groups of pink-skinned tourists, all happy and excited, heading in the opposite direction, back to their hotels. *They wouldn't be so happy later tonight*, I thought, once those sunburns had a chance to settle in.

I stayed on the beach side of Kalakaua and then jaywalked across to the other side of the street when I got down near Kapahulu Avenue. The setting sun was beginning to sink beneath the water, off to my right, as I passed by Waikiki Beach. It looked like a giant, glowing beach ball, just sitting there, far out on the horizon. A warm, beautiful day was about to turn into a warm, beautiful evening.

When I got home, I took a shower and popped a TV dinner into the microwave. Julien, my boyfriend from France, was gone, spending a few days on the North Shore, shacked up with some surfer girl he'd met at the beach. That was okay with me – we had that kind of open relationship. He fucked who he wanted and I fucked – and sucked – who I wanted and, occasionally, we got together and fucked each other. It was the perfect arrangement, both from his point of view and from mine.

I really liked Julien. And I liked it when he fucked me, too. He had a thick, slightly-curved dick that filled my pussy nicely and he had a big nose that he also … well, that's not really relevant to this story. I'll tell you about his nose tricks some other time.

Whatever. Julien wasn't here now and I wasn't particularly horny, anyway. I ate and then turned on the TV to watch the evening news and get the latest info on a story that had dominated local news for nearly a week, the abduction of local teacher, Glenna Biggle – ostensibly by aliens. The kind that come from other planets.

According to Miss Biggle, she had been abducted by aliens and taken aboard a UFO, where she was held captive and repeatedly sexually assaulted. The local paper and TV news weren't giving a lot of details and were treating the UFO part of the story as something of a joke, but the internet was abuzz with stories of interspecies sex and non-stop orgies. Headlines such as, "Hawaiian Woman Survives Days of Non-Stop Alien Rape!" and "UFO Sex Orgies!" crowded out tales of government corruption and impending climate disaster. My favorite, though, was, "UFO Abductee Claims Alien Sex Was *Absolutely Wonderful!*" Good to know, I suppose, if I ever meet an alien.

Miss Biggle's story had caused a sensation in Honolulu and, thanks to social media, had spread to the mainland and around the world. According to the official story, she was missing for three days, during which an island-wide search turned up no trace of her, so the search was called off. Then, on the fourth day, she was discovered, naked and disoriented, wandering in Waikiki. She had a smile on her face and was covered in a powdery, silvery substance which scientists apparently were having a hard time identifying.

When questioned by those who found her about what had happened, she told a fantastic story about being abducted by aliens she called 'Silvers,' taken aboard a space ship and held captive there. And when asked what had happened while she was aboard the alien vessel, she reportedly claimed that, for much of the time she was there, various aliens took turns 'fucking her silly!' That last part, by the way, came from a story I read online, not from the local news, so, ... you know.

Anyway, my two favorite news announcers, Horace and his female co-anchor, Jennifer or Jessica or something like that, were bantering back and forth, just as they always did.

"Well, I don't know, Jane," Horace was saying. "This whole aliens from outer space thing seems just a little hard to believe, don't you think?"

Jane. Her name was Jane. I watch these guys almost every night – I should know that.

"Maybe it is, Horace," Jane said. "But Miss Biggle is sticking to her story. Did you know that she has been interviewed, under *hypnosis,* by two local psychologists?"

"Really? I hadn't heard that. And? What did they say? Do they believe her?"

Jane gave Horace one of those I-know-something-you-don't smiles and said, "They both agreed that *something* unusual happened to her and that she *believes* she was kidnapped – abducted – by these 'Silvers,' as she calls them. But they can't positively conclude that what she believes is what actually happened."

Horace snorted. "Just like a shrink, Jane. All wishy-washy. Never give you a straight answer. And hypnosis is really an unproven therapy, you know."

I tuned them out as they drifted off on a tangent about the benefits, or lack thereof, of hypnosis. You know – whether or not it really worked. I leaned back, my eyelids began to droop and I was almost asleep when I thought I heard one of them say something that caused me to sit up straight, instantly awake. "What?" I said to my TV. "What did you say?"

Not getting the requested answer from the TV, I grabbed my remote, rewound the segment for a few seconds and replayed it. And I was right. One of them – it was Jane – had said what I thought I'd heard. UAPIG was coming to town.

Chapter 3

UAPIG. The <u>U</u>nidentified <u>A</u>erial <u>P</u>henomena <u>I</u>nvestigative <u>G</u>roup. An unfortunate acronym, perhaps, but they were the country's second-leading UFO research organization. According to Jane, UAPIG was expected to arrive the following morning to conduct an interview with Miss Biggle and to investigate the purported abduction site for possible physical evidence. And if UAPIG was coming to Honolulu, that meant their chief investigator, Professor Maynard Krebzinski, was coming, too.

I almost had an orgasm, right there on my couch, when I heard the news. Famed ufologist Maynard Krebzinski was coming to Honolulu! While I wasn't that big a fan of UFOs or UFO conspiracy theories, I was a *ginormous* fan of Professor Krebs, as he was called. In my mind, he was the perfect dork – the number one guy at the top of my secret mental list entitled, *Guys I Want to Blow!*

He'd been there for at least a couple of years. Leading my list, I mean. Ever since I first saw him on some late-night talk show, explaining to the smirking host what UAPIG was, what they did, and why *everyone* should believe in flying saucers from outer space.

He was just incredibly dorky, from his face to the clothes he wore to the way he seemed utterly unaware the guy doing the interview was mocking him. He had kinky red hair, faded and thinning somewhat with age. It stood out, unevenly, from his head, making it look as if it was planning an escape. Think of an older Albert Einstein with red hair.

In addition to the clown hairdo, Professor Krebs was slightly on the portly side and had freckles. Lots and lots of freckles. And a big, silly-looking, lopsided grin, too. And, at least that first time I saw him, he was wearing a yellow shirt, a red bow tie, and a green sport jacket. I never did get a chance to see what he was wearing below his waist, but it wouldn't have surprised me at all if his feet had been encased in giant purple clown shoes. As I watched him that time, I remembered seeing photos of a 1950's era children's show character, a marionette named *Howdy Doody*, and thinking that's who Professor Krebs really was – Howdy Doody, grown into middle-age.

Yes, the professor was heading my list. Number one with a bullet. Of all the dicks in all the world, his was the one I most wanted to suck. For a long time, it had seemed an impossible dream, what with me being in Honolulu and him heading up the UAPIG research facility, located in Virginia. But now it seemed I might have a chance to make that impossible dream come true. All I had to do was figure out where he was going to be staying and then arrange to meet him. That seemed like an easy enough task for a clever girl like me.

I leaned back and closed my eyes, imagining what it would be like if I could arrange some alone-time with super-hot Professor Krebs. Don't laugh. That's the way I thought of him. *Super-hot!* And yeah, that cock of his wouldn't stand a chance if I could get him all to myself for a couple of hours. I'd drain that fuck-stick of his so completely he wouldn't be able to get it up for a month. And although I didn't know now what his favorite song was, once I found out, I'd hum it for him. I'd hum and hum and he'd cum and cum and then I'd hum some more. I smiled to myself as a picture of what that might look like slowly formed in my mind.

And then I nodded off. I suppose I shouldn't have closed my eyes, but I did and I just fell asleep. Not too surprising, I guess. A long afternoon of sucking cock can actually be quite tiring, you know. Enjoyable. But tiring.

It was almost nine when I woke up. The apartment was dark, my neck was stiff, and I had to pee. I turned on the light and stumbled into the bathroom, massaging my neck along the way.

There was a lot to be done before Professor Krebs and the UAPIG investigative team arrived the following morning. I needed to find out where they were going to stay and what the professor's schedule was going to be, so that I could arrange an *accidental* meeting between us. Fortunately, there was the internet for that.

My laptop under my arm and a bottle of Coke in my hand, I returned to the living room, settled back onto my couch and went to the UAPIG homepage, which I'd conveniently bookmarked long ago. Although my interest in UFOs was minimal, I visited this page frequently, just to see the friendly, freckly face of Professor Krebs smiling at me, courtesy of a large head shot that filled most of the page. Just staring at that beautiful face for a minute or so was enough to get me all horny and super wet. But this was no time for masturbating – I had work to do.

I scrolled through the various pages until I came to the one I was looking for – *Upcoming Events*. And there it was, just a small blurb next to a tiny thumbnail of the professor. *To celebrate the release of his 17th book, <u>Angels from Outer Space,</u> Professor Krebzinski will be appearing for a book reading and signing event at the Pakaka'i Bookshop in Honolulu, Hawai'i, at 8 PM on the 12th of this month.*

That's all it said. Oh, sure, there were other dates and other book readings listed, but those were all in Des Moines, Iowa or Pine Bluffs, Arkansas or someplace else too far away for me to attend. And there was no mention of Glenna Biggle, silver aliens, or an impending investigation, which meant I wasn't able to find out the professor's schedule or where he'd be staying. So, it looked as if the only way I'd be able to meet him was to show up tomorrow night – the 12th – at the Pakaka'i Bookshop.

Chapter 4

The Pakaka'i Bookshop was located on Smith Street, just around the corner from Hotel Street, in downtown Honolulu. I hadn't been down here in years and, ordinarily, I'd *never* come down here after dark. It was kind of a creepy area, in my opinion, full of bars and tattoo parlors and lots of dangerous-looking people, both men and women. And, although it was claimed the place had been cleaned up in recent years, it still seemed like the kind of place where a reasonably good-looking young woman – me, for example – could find herself getting kidnapped and raped. And I *really* wasn't into that!

I'd taken the bus from Waikiki – I don't own a car – and had arrived early. So I stood outside, on the sidewalk, looking at the books displayed in the window and just killing time, not wanting to be the first one to arrive at the professor's book-signing party. At 8:02, I went inside, fashionably late.

The shop was long and narrow, brightly lit, clean, and exuded something of a *cheerful* vibe, not something I was expecting from a store in this part of town. Professor Krebs didn't seem to be around, but down at the far end, a man and a woman were setting up chairs around a table stacked with hardcover books. A crowd of roughly twenty people stood around, watching, apparently waiting for the couple to finish their task so they could take seats. I wandered over in that direction.

"What's going on?" I said to the woman who was setting up chairs.

The woman, thin and severe-looking, her gray hair tied back in a bun, stopped what she was doing and looked at me. "Professor

Krebzinski is about to give a reading from his new book, his *wonderful* new book, *Angels from Outer Space*."

"You don't say."

"Oh, but I do," she said, giving me a cold, professional smile. "Have a seat. I'm sure you'll enjoy hearing what he has to say."

"All right. Perhaps I will. And thank you."

She nodded and went back to her task, opening and arranging folding chairs. When she and her partner were finished, they disappeared through a door in the back while the small crowd scrambled to get seats near the front. I took a seat at the rear.

A couple of minutes went by and then the door in the back opened and the man himself, Professor Maynard Krebzinski, appeared, smiling and waving. He was dressed more conservatively than that time I'd first seen him on TV but he was still wearing an oversized red bow tie and a striped yellow shirt. As I watched him walk toward the table in front, it occurred to me that there was only one possible explanation for the rainbow colors of the man's wardrobe – he was color-blind!

The small crowd clapped enthusiastically as he pulled out a chair and sat down behind the table. This was the first time I'd ever seen him in person and I was impressed with how much better he looked than he did on the website photo. Not quite as pudgy-looking. And it appeared he had combed his hair sometime in the past few days. He was really, *really* cute. Not conventionally cute, I'll admit. More like circus-clown cute. But cute is cute, right?

Professor Krebs talked to the crowd in a friendly manner, explaining how he came to write the book, the research that went into it, and a bunch of other boring stuff. Boring to me, anyway. I wasn't here because I was a fan of the professor's writing or his research methods, and I wasn't really all that interested in UFOs, either. The attraction for me was in finding out what the good professor was hiding in his pants!

The rest of the crowd seemed to be eating this stuff up, though. When Professor Krebs was finished with his introductory remarks and had read a fairly lengthy excerpt from his book, he asked if there were any questions. About a hundred hands went up. Pretty impressive, when you consider there were only about 20 people in the crowd.

Anyway, the professor answered questions, sold and signed books, and people began to leave. I hung back until I was the last of the crowd and then approached the table. "Got any books left?" I said, smiling at him and eyeing the six or seven books still on the table.

He gave me a quick once-over. "For you, absolutely," he said, and smiled back.

The price of the book was $27.95. I handed him $28 and said, "Keep the change."

He smiled at me again. "Wow. A tip. Thanks."

Damn, he was *so* cute. "I wish it was more."

"Name?" he said, picking up his pen and opening a book.

"Terry Jean. Two words, Terry with a Y."

"You a big fan of aliens?" he said, scribbling something onto the title page.

"Oh, sure," I lied. "Big, big fan."

I guess he sensed I was lying. He stopped writing and gave me a quizzical look. "Really?"

"Of course. Why else would I be here?"

"Well, you could have come just to see me," he said with a sly smile.

Fuck! The man was flirting with me, right here in the bookstore. This was working out great!

I walked around the table until I was standing next to him, then put my hand on his shoulder and leaned forward, pretending to be interested in what he was writing. "Maybe I did," I said. "Maybe I'm a Maynard Krebzinski groupie."

"That would be interesting. I don't think groupies have ever been a problem for me."

"Problem? Having groupies wouldn't be *that* much of a problem, would it?"

"Well, never having had any, I wouldn't know," he said. "So, Terry Jean, do you have a favorite alien species?"

Uh-oh. Specifics. I knew I should have prepared more for this encounter. I searched my brain, trying to come up with some names of aliens, but not much popped up.

"I like those little gray ones, of course," I said, finally. "I guess everyone has them near the top of their lists. And I'm *really* interested in those new ones I recently heard about. The Silvers, I think they're called."

"Ah, yes. The Silvers. A brand-new species, one we haven't encountered before. I'm intrigued by them, as well. In fact, that's one of the reasons I came here, to Honolulu, you know. To investigate that recently-reported abduction by Silvers."

"I heard," I said.

"So, what is it that interests you about this new species – the Silvers?"

This was it – the opening I'd been waiting for. *It's now or never, Terry Jean. Make your play.* I leaned over and dropped my hand lightly into his lap and whispered in his ear, "I hear they have big, juicy, delicious dicks!" I told him.

And that's when the lady who'd been setting up chairs returned, saying, "C'mon, Maynard, we have to leave or we'll be late."

I don't know what I'd expected to happen. There wasn't much I could accomplish, right there in the Pakaka'i Bookshop. A few people were still hanging around, examining books, even though it was past the store's official closing time. It wasn't as if I could crawl under the table and give the professor's dick a big, sloppy slurpee, right there on the spot, and no one would notice. Although I'm not sure what I might have done if the store had been empty. Still, having the chair lady show up was a major bummer!

Professor Krebs gave me a reluctant smile. "That's my handler," he said, ignoring my comment about tasty dicks. "She keeps me on schedule. I have to leave."

"You have a *handler*?"

"Unfortunately, I do."

"Damn!" I said.

He stood up to leave, then leaned over and wrote some additional comments in the book he was autographing for me. "Here," he said, handing it to me.

I noticed for the first time that his pants, which I'd thought were black, were actually a dark purple color, and right now, as he was preparing to leave, the crotch area was exhibiting a noticeable bulge. "Damn," I said again. "I was hoping –"

"C'mon, Maynard. Let's go. We don't want to be late," said the professor's handler, cutting me off.

"I really have to go," he said. And then, just before he turned and headed for the back door, he added, "Be sure to read what I wrote in your book."

"I will," I said as he walked away. And I did. It read, *For sweet and beautiful Terry Jean. So glad to have you as a fan!* And it was signed, *Krebs.*

That was nice. He called me 'sweet,' which wasn't the way I usually thought of myself but it was nice to receive, as a compliment, from someone else. However, it was what he'd written beneath his autograph that caught my attention. In block letters it said, *Room 614, Kamaloha Surf Hotel, 8 PM tomorrow ???*

One question mark would have been plenty, Krebs. I smiled as I watched him disappear through the door. *I'll be there!*

Oh, bummer. That's the end of this sample of <u>The Man from UAPIG</u>. *I wonder if TJ will manage to get some significant alone time with the*

professor. I'm sure she will. But then what? Will things work out the way she hopes? Or will the professor be too busy with his UFO investigation for a little fun-in-the-sack time? Only one way to find out – download the book from your favorite online bookseller.

Meanwhile, here's a sample from another one of my ongoing series. These stories are best described as erotic – <u>highly</u> erotic – romances. This sample is the opening of book one.

Jennifer's Story
Pleasantly Plump (sample)

"I am *not* fat!" I told my full-length bathroom mirror as I climbed out of the shower. I'd caught it staring at me.

This is the part where, in the movies, the mirror answers back and says something like, "Well, *I* certainly didn't say anything." But my mirror evidently had no acting skills. It just sat there, staring at me, never saying a word.

"I'm soft and curvy, with beautiful, full titties, a nice, round ass, and a pussy that deserves way better than I get from David," I continued, repeating the affirmation I'd written for myself and was now required to repeat at least 10 times a day, according to the online *Pussy Power* course I was taking.

Every word of that affirmation was true. A lot of guys would put me in the category known as *Pretty Fucking Hot*, I was sure. But not David. With him it was always, *Hey, babe, why don't you try to lose a few pounds?* or, *You putting on weight, sweetie?* frequently followed by a slap on the ass.

And all because of an extra five or ten pounds of baby fat. Hell, I'm only 20 years old. In a couple of years that will be gone, as if by magic, and I'll be just about perfect. Which is what David wants, apparently.

I've never really understood that. Why some guys are so into screwing those skinny, bony model-types, I mean. That couldn't be a lot of fun for either of them, clanging their hip bones together as they pumped away. You'd think those guys would rather be lying on a soft, warm body with a little padding. Like mine.

Anyway, if *wham-bam-thank-you-ma'am* David was doing the screwing, there wasn't much to worry about, I guess. He was seldom in the saddle long enough to do any real damage. That thought brought a smile to my lips as I got dressed, followed by a frown as I realized that's all I ever really got from him – a quickie. David was almost always a quick, unsatisfying fuck, at least for me.

Too bad he couldn't be more like Alejandro. Alejandro knew how to treat a woman, both in and out of bed. He was kind and gentle, as well as being tall, dark and mysterious, muscular, and handsome. And, best of all, perhaps, he was equipped with eight inches of the smoothest, most beautiful, most delicious man-meat possible – a cock that would more than satisfy just about any girl.

Only trouble was, Alejandro wasn't real. He was a sweet vision, existing only in my head, a guy I'd invented years ago. He was the guy I imagined each time I gave my vibrator a workout.

Yeah, my vibrator, my wonderful vibrator. A vibrating dildo, actually. The only time my pussy ever got any real action was when I broke out that old, eight-inch fake cock I bought myself for my nineteenth birthday. I ordered it online and didn't realize how long it was. And *thick*, too. That little jewel took some getting used to – a thick eight inches was a tight fit. But it fits better now, thanks to lots of practice over the past year or so. Which reminded me – I needed to replace it. The silicone was beginning to peel off from overuse.

I'd definitely gotten my money's worth from it, though. Maybe I'll order the six-speed, 10-inch monster dong, this time, I thought. That's the one with the little clit-rubbing extension on one side and a mini-dick sticking out the other side, so you can fuck yourself in the pussy and the ass at the same time, if you want to. I'm not sure I'll be using it that way on a regular basis, but I'll definitely give it a try because I once had a guy stick his finger up my ass while he was pounding my pussy and I came almost immediately. That was one of the best orgasms I ever had!

My phone rang and I picked it up. "Hey, what's up?" I said to my best friend, Marlene. We've been friends since elementary school and she calls me two or three mornings a week at about this time, to "check in," as she phrases it, but I sometimes think she calls me just to see if I'm still alive.

"Wha'cha doin'?" she said.

"Nothing. Getting dressed. Talking to my mirror."

"Yeah? About what?"

"You know – David, guys, the fact that I haven't had a good screwing in over a month. That kind of shit."

Marlene laughed. "I can't believe a dick-friendly girl like you can't find a guy to give her a good fuck."

"What makes you think I'm *that* dick-friendly?"

"You like dicks, don't you?"

"Well, duh! Of course. Where would the world be without dicks?" I said, laughing.

"That makes you dick-friendly. If you like them, you have to be friendly to them."

It was tough to argue with that logic. "I guess," I said.

"So, listen, you wanna go to a flick tonight?"

"Can't. I've got a date with David."

"Oh." Marlene didn't much care for David. Although she'd never actually told me she didn't like him, I could tell from the way she reacted whenever I mentioned him that she thought I could do better.

"Maybe some other night?" I suggested. "This is more like a business meeting than a date. Some college friend of David's is moving here and David wants to help him buy a house, or rent an apartment, or something. So the three of us are going out for drinks." David was a real estate agent, so this was both a business meeting and a college reunion of sorts.

"Yeah, okay. Some other night, then. Anyway, I gotta go. Just wanted to check in."

"I'm still alive," I told her.

"That's good," she said, and hung up.

I finished dressing and headed off to school, where I was already five minutes late for my psych class.

David showed up at eight, right on time, as always. "Ready?" he said.

"Yup. Let's go." I turned off my lights and we headed down the steps to his car.

"You look nice tonight," he said, as he opened the car door and held it for me.

Whoa! What the fuck was that? A compliment from David – I must have misheard him. I've worn this outfit a dozen times before and he's never said a word about it. "Thanks," I said, climbing in. "You look nice, too."

He grinned and closed the door, then got in the other side and we left, heading for – well, I didn't know where we were going. David hadn't mentioned it.

"Where's this friend of yours? I thought he was going to have drinks with us."

"Yeah, he is. Al – that's his name, Al – said he'd meet us there."

Al? Could that be short for Alejandro? I smiled inwardly at the thought. "Where's *there*? Where are we going?" I said.

"Dottie's. I told him we'd meet him there at around eight-thirty."

Of course. Dottie's Den, David's favorite bar and grille. Tiny little tables with tiny little lamps putting out so little illumination you couldn't see the high prices on the menu. Watery drinks, crappy food and rude, snarky servers – what's not to like? Plus, there was an overall *damp* feeling to the place. I hated it.

We got there early – Dottie's was only 10 or 12 blocks from my place. The dining room was pretty much empty, about normal for a weekday night. We skipped through to the lounge, also just about empty, and grabbed a booth with a view of the entrance. I've always wondered how this place stays in business. Every time we've been here it's been like this – empty. Of course, we always come during the week because David is so busy on weekends, what with open houses and stuff. They probably did a shitload of business on weekends, was my guess.

"What's this friend of yours look like?" I said, after we'd ordered and our drinks had come.

"He's tall. Dark. He's from Mexico, I think. Or Columbia. Someplace in South America. Yeah, Columbia, maybe."

"Don't you know? I thought you were friends."

"Yeah, well, more like acquaintances, really. I know him from school and he knows I'm in real estate, so he contacted me."

Hmm. Tall, dark, and Hispanic. Just like Alejandro. I took a big gulp of the illegally-served, watery screwdriver in front of me and began to fantasize about the mysterious Al from Mexico. Or Columbia. Or someplace in South America.

"That's him," David said, interrupting my reverie.

I looked up and practically choked. The large, muscular man walking toward us with a huge smile on his dark face looked almost exactly like my fantasy man – the man who filled my thoughts while I rode my dildo – Alejandro.

Fuck! Was this possible? Maybe I was dreaming. Yeah, that had to be it. I fell asleep on my couch, waiting for David, and now I was dreaming. But I wasn't dreaming, so I stood up, along with David, to greet him.

David introduced us. "Al Entavez, this is my main squeeze, Jennifer," he said.

That really pissed me off. Him calling me his 'main squeeze,' I mean. I wasn't anybody's 'squeeze,' main or otherwise. Least of all David's. David was just a temporary distraction, someone who was supposed to make me happy for a while and then move on. And he wasn't doing a very good job of it.

"Well, *hel-lo*, Jennifer," Al said, taking my hand in his. He stepped back and took a good long look at me, eyeing me from head to toe as David looked on, beaming. A weak feeling slid into my knees.

"David told me he was bringing his girlfriend tonight," Al continued, "but he failed to mention she was a model. A *very* beautiful model." That weak feeling left my knees and slithered up my inner thighs.

"Always the kidder," David commented, sitting back down.

Fuck you, David.

Al was still standing there, holding my hand in his and eyeballing me in a decidedly non-kidding manner. I could feel the warmth creeping up my neck and knew I was blushing, so I did the only thing I could think of. I shook his hand, said, "Thank you for the compliment, Al," and sat back down.

"Call me Alex," he said, sitting down beside me. "I prefer that to Al."

Alex. All right. I'd been hoping that Al was short for Alejandro, but what the hell – Alex was a perfectly nice name. I was also a little disappointed that Alex had no noticeable accent. He sounded like an American. The Alex of my fantasies – whoops, I meant the *Alejandro* of my fantasies – always told me how hot I was in a really sexy Hispanic accent. Oh, well, as the song goes, *You Can't Always Get What You Want.*

David didn't waste any time rehashing their college years or catching up on more recent events in their lives – he got right to work. "So, you're looking for a place here in Orlando, huh? You wanna rent or buy?"

Alex turned his attention away from me and toward the task at hand – finding a place to live. "I guess I'd like to rent for about a year, get used to the community, you know, then buy a place."

"Excellent way to go about it," David said. "I can help you with that."

I sipped my drink and tuned them out, losing myself in fantasies about Alex. Or Alejandro. I wasn't sure which of them I was daydreaming about, since the two men were practically identical, but I was just getting to a good part when David's phone rang, snapping me back to reality.

"What, now?" I heard him say, followed by a period of silence. Then, "Shit, Joan, it's almost nine o'clock. I'm in a bar."

A longer silent period followed, presumably while Joan, the office manager at David's company, explained whatever had caused this interruption.

"All right, all right. Fifteen minutes," he said, and hung up.

"Something wrong?" Alex said.

"Crap! I'm sorry – I've gotta go to the office."

"Now?" both Alex and I said at the same time.

"Yeah. Look, I'll only be gone a half-hour. I've just gotta sign some papers that need to be delivered by eight o'clock tomorrow morning. Take me two minutes and then I'll come right back. You guys just stay here, have a couple of drinks, get to know one another or whatever, and I'll be back before you know it. Okay?"

Alex tossed a quick, smiling glance in my direction, then turned back to David and said, "Sure. No problem." I nodded my agreement, as if I really had a say in what David intended to do.

"Great, then." He drained his glass, offered us a final, "I'll be back in a jif," and left.

And that's the end of the sample of <u>Jennifer's Story.</u> Darn! Just when it was starting to get interesting, too. I'd be willing to bet that leaving Jennifer and Alex alone at Dottie's Den turns out to be a bad move for David, but ... who knows? You can find out by downloading the book.

Here's another sample for you. This one is from my <u>Mike and Melanie Escapades</u> series, an examination into the swinging lifestyle of a young, unmarried couple in their twenties. I like to think of these stories as non-stop nasty! I'll bet you'll agree.

Valentine Surprise
A Mike and Melanie Escapade, Book 1
(Sample)

"We'll meet in the bedroom at nine o'clock, okay? But you have to be in there 15 minutes early. And no peeking out."

"Sounds like a plan," Mike said. "I'll be there, waiting for my surprise."

"You're gonna like this one, I promise," I told him.

"I always like your surprises, Mel. You know that."

"Yeah, but this is gonna be the best one ever. By far!"

He laughed at my enthusiasm and went back to watching the news on TV. I started fixing dinner while I thought about how Mike would react to his 'surprise.' Surprises were a fun game Mike and I had been playing for the past year or so. Usually they were just little sex things, like an extra-sloppy blowjob for Mike. Or like the time he bought me an eight-inch long, extra-thick, silicone dildo and then fucked me with it. But I had something special planned for this evening, something that had taken me a lot of effort to arrange. My college roommate and long-time friend, Susan, was coming over to help me treat Mike to a Valentine's Day surprise – a threesome.

It had taken a bit of arm-twisting to get her to agree. Well, ... not really, now that I think about it. In fact, I think the first time I brought it up she said something like, "Mike? You mean, your hunky old man with the big dick?"

And I said, "He's not old. He's 28. And how do you know how big his dick is?"

"You told me."

"Oh, yeah. I guess I did mention he has a nice, big dick."

"About 400 times."

I stuck my tongue out at her. "So, how about it?"

"Sure. He's a hunk. I've always wanted to fuck Mike – I've told you so." That she had. It was the reason I'd been confident Susie would agree to my plans for a threesome. And so we'd made plans to double-team him on Valentine's Day.

They called her 'Susie the Slut' back when we were in school, a nickname she well-deserved. She was a pretty blonde with big, natural boobs, a nice round ass and a really *friendly* attitude toward dicks. We weren't exactly roommates – we shared a two-bedroom apartment off campus. I had my own bedroom and Susie had hers, and hers had frequent visitors. *Lots* of them!

But that was then and this is now. And tonight, Susie was going to be the visitor. I had my fingers mentally crossed that everything would work out the way we'd planned it.

After dinner, Mike went into the den to do something on the computer. Watch porn, probably. That was good preparation for the evening's upcoming activities, I thought. *Get nice and horny, Mike. Susie the Slut and I are going to screw you silly!*

I took control of the TV and spent some time channel surfing but was unable to find anything that interested me. Other things were on my mind. I was worried that Susie might not show up on time or, worse yet, might not show up at all. And as the clock inched closer to ten to nine, the time she was supposed to arrive, my apprehension grew.

At quarter to nine, Mike kissed me on the forehead, said, "I'll be waiting," then disappeared into the bedroom and closed the door. At least step one was going off on schedule, I thought. That was a good omen.

Ten to nine came and went. And no Susie. I wondered if I should call her and see what happened, but while I was thinking about it, my doorbell rang. I breathed a sigh of relief and padded to the door. "I was starting to get worried," I said as I opened the door.

Only, it wasn't Susie standing there on my front porch. Well, that's not right – she *was* there. But she wasn't alone. There was a guy on the porch with her.

"You brought a date?!!" I said.

"Not exactly. I showed up alone, but he was already here."

I looked more closely at the guy standing next to her. "Jerry?"

"Hi, Mel," he said.

"What are you doing here?" Jerry was Mike's basketball buddy. The two of them played almost every Sunday afternoon in pickup games at a church gym where Jerry was a part-time custodian. He was something of a stud, tall and muscular and rumored to have a giant-sized cock, and I'd fantasized about fucking him more than a few times.

"Uh, Mike asked me to come over. Something about a ... a surprise." Even in the dim light on the porch, I could see Jerry was blushing – he obviously knew more about the 'surprise' than he was letting on.

I almost burst out laughing as it suddenly dawned on me what was happening – Mike had seen me flirting with Jerry a couple of times and had decided to set us up, as his surprise for me. "Come in, come in," I said.

The three of us settled into the living room. "You two know each other?" I asked Susie.

"We met on your front porch, Mel. So, ... yeah, we've met."

"Okay, let me go get Mike. Be right back." I left to inform Mike of what was happening.

He was lying on the bed, watching TV. "Is it time?" he said.

"Change of plans. We've got company."

He grinned, obviously knowing Jerry was scheduled to appear. "Really? What happened?"

"Come out into the living room and see," I said, turning to leave. "I'm gonna make drinks."

"Break out that wine I bought last week."

"Yeah, okay." I went back to the living room, where Susie and Jerry had made themselves comfortable on our sofa. "Drinks?" I said and, without waiting for an answer, proceeded to open the pinot noir Mike had requested.

Mike came padding out of the bedroom, saying, "Hi, guys," and joining us. He didn't seem surprised to see Susie and, of course, he knew Jerry would be there since he'd invited him.

"See that bowl on the coffee table? The marbly one?" I said to Susie.

"Yeah."

"Open it."

She pulled the top off the bowl and peered inside. "Hey, weed! And some of it is all rolled up, ready to go. Great."

"Yeah, light a couple," I told her. "There are lighters in that other bowl."

Susie torched a couple of joints and sent one down the sofa for me to share with Mike, who was sitting on the floor, on a *zabuton*. We sat smoking and sipping our wine for a while, not really talking much. The situation was awkward. We all knew why we were here, together – at least, we all knew to some degree – but none of us seemed to know how to get things started and conversation was on the light side.

"This is nice," Jerry said. "This weed, I mean. It's nice and smooth, not harsh. I like it."

"Yeah, I bought it last week," Mike said. "It's called *Beautiful Dream*."

We all agreed it was 'nice.' And then the conversation lagged again.

Eventually, Mike said to me, "By the way, whatever happened to that big surprise you promised me? It's long after nine o'clock. Almost ten."

I took a big hit off the joint, held it for a few seconds, then blew it out in the direction of Susie. "It's sitting right there," I said, pointing at her.

Susie flashed a big grin at Mike and said, "Hel-lo, Mike, my man. Surprise, surprise. Why don't you come up here and sit next to me?" She stood up and swapped places with me, telling me to, "Scoot over there, next to Jerry."

So I moved over, close to Jerry. Real close. And when I looked back, Mike was already sitting on the sofa and Susie was straddling his lap, sucking his face and giving him a little bit of a forward-facing lapdance. That was quick! Leave it to Susie to get this train rolling.

"Looks like they're having fun," Jerry said.

I watched them for a few seconds. "Yeah, that does look like fun," I agreed. I leaned up and kissed him, at the same time dropping my hand into his lap, not really surprised to find something hard hiding inside his shorts.

"Hey, I'm going to give Susie a tour of the house," Mike suddenly announced, temporarily interrupting my attempt to get something going with Jerry.

"Fine," I told him. "Make sure you show her the bedroom."

"Oh, I will. Don't worry." The two of them headed off in the direction of our bedroom, and I went back to what I'd been doing – kissing Jerry. So maybe Mike's threesome wasn't going to work out tonight. But I was sure he wasn't going to be disappointed. Susie had lots of experience and I was sure Mike was going to have a good time.

And I was going to have a good time, too. At least, I hoped so. I broke my kiss with Jerry and said, "Mike told me you have a king-sized cock. Is that true?"

He looked embarrassed. "It's, ... uh, yeah, it's pretty big."

"Can I see?"

"If you want to."

"Oh, I do," I said, smiling at him. "I definitely do."

"Help yourself," he said.

I unbuttoned the front of his shorts, which were tenting big time, and unzipped his fly. "Something big is in there," I said, stating the obvious.

He didn't say anything, he just grinned.

I reached in and pulled it out. Ever heard the term, *monster dick*? That's what popped out of Jerry's pants – a humongous monster of a dick. It looked delicious. I stroked it slowly up and down with one hand. It wasn't only long, it was thick. "Damn, Jerry, that's a big one!" I said.

And that's the end of the sample of <u>Valentine Surprise: A Mike and Melanie Escapade, Book 1</u>. I wonder what Mel's going to do, now that Jerry's monster has been released from its cage. I have a pretty good idea but I don't want to give the fun away. You can find out by downloading the book and reading it.

Well, that's it. I hope you enjoyed the book and the previews. If you haven't done so already, please don't forget to leave a review for this book, *The Waikiki Hummer.* See ya soon, I hope!

Shannon